LAST VIOLENT CALL

ALSO BY CHLOE GONG

THE SECRET SHANGHAI SERIES:
**THESE VIOLENT DELIGHTS
OUR VIOLENT ENDS
FOUL LADY FORTUNE**

LAST VIOLENT CALL

CHLOE GONG

HODDERSCAPE

First published in Great Britain in 2023 by Hodder & Stoughton
An Hachette UK company

1

Copyright © Chloe Gong 2023

A CIP catalogue record for this title is available from the British Library

Hardback ISBN 978 1 399 71252 1
Trade Paperback ISBN 978 1 399 71253 8
eBook ISBN 978 1 399 71254 5

Printed and bound in Great Britain by Clays Ltd, Elcograf S.p.A.

Hodder & Stoughton policy is to use papers that are natural, renewable and
recyclable products and made from wood grown in sustainable forests. The logging
and manufacturing processes are expected to conform to the environmental
regulations of the country of origin.

Hodder & Stoughton Ltd
Carmelite House
50 Victoria Embankment
London EC4Y 0DZ

www.hodder.co.uk

Contents

A
FOUL
THING

FOR JULIETTE AND ROMA

1

SEPTEMBER 1931

Two knocks meant "all clear," and three knocks meant "dorogaya, for the love of God, I'm holding something in my hands." The announcement system had been put into place at the front door because Juliette Cai had a bad habit of launching herself at her husband each time he came back into the house, even if he had merely been away for a few hours getting groceries. It was by a combination of sheer luck and trained dexterity that Roma had once managed to catch her with one hand and not drop the bag of pears in his other.

The footsteps outside grew louder. In the kitchen, the sunflower-shaped clock struck four in the afternoon. Roma had estimated he would be arriving home today around this time. He had only gone to the next town over.

As Juliette peered up from her desk, however, she didn't quickly push her chair back to await Roma's knock. Their house was one of the many low-ceilinged residences in Zhouzhuang that pressed right to the edge of a thin canal. Some mornings, when there were boats moving along the thoroughfare, Juliette would be awoken by the soft echo of lapping water. She would pad outside still in her nightclothes, early enough that the sun was barely peeking over the houses on the other side of the canal, their ceramic roof tiles cast in gentle gold, curved slopes lit by refractions bouncing off the languid water. Chirping birds and brisk air, heightened by the absolute quiet permeating the township at such an hour.

But theirs was also the only residence on the outer side of the township's farthest canal, before everything turned to water and wet forestry. Where the inner side comprised a row of houses with frequently open doors and chatty neighbors, it was a rare occasion that anyone would cross the tall stone bridge to walk along the outer path instead—unless it was to approach the house tucked beside the weeping willow tree, the house with the windows that had been refurbished with bulletproof glass, the house rumored to be owned by former city gangsters.

So when Juliette heard a scuffle against the house exterior, she unsheathed the knife strapped to her leg and marched to the door, swinging it right open.

The stranger barely had a second to flinch before she leveled the blade at his throat.

"I *told* you to walk behind me. I should let my wife slice you up just for being a nuisance."

The voice rang from some distance away, a figure crossing the canal bridge with his hands in his pockets. He had started speaking long before he saw the scene in front of him, because Roma Montagov knew that Juliette could isolate the sound of his steps, and she wouldn't take kindly to the ones that were not his.

"Thankfully"—Roma hopped off the bridge and walked over, then tapped Juliette's elbow when he was close enough—"she is ever so peace-loving and benevolent."

Graciously, Juliette withdrew her blade, giving the stranger a smile. He seemed young, surely no older than seventeen, wearing a gray shirt that was nicer than the usual quality around these parts.

"Tea?" she asked.

"Oh my God," the boy whispered under his breath, eyes wide in shock. "You almost killed me."

"Untrue." Juliette was already retreating back into the house, turning her papers over as she passed her desk. She proceeded into the kitchen, kicking a log out of the way so that it pressed closer to the unlit fireplace. With the practiced swiftness of routine, she put the kettle on the stove and withdrew three teacups from the cupboard, setting them on the painted blue table. "You would be long dead if I were trying to kill you."

Roma ushered the boy through the kitchen entryway. He pulled a chair out at the dining table; the boy sat down heavily. As the kettle started to whine, Juliette took the boiling water off the heat in tandem to Roma reaching for the tea leaves on the counter. He dropped them into the cups from the left as she poured from the right, the two crisscrossing in the middle, where Roma leaned in to press a kiss to her cheek.

"Did you have a good three days without me?" he asked, switching to Russian. At the other end of the table, the boy stayed quiet, but he had sat up straighter with a note of curiosity. It didn't seem like he understood Roma's words, but he was trying very hard to follow anyway.

"I was bored out of my mind," Juliette replied, switching as well. "I think I finished all our invoice work within the first five hours and turned to organizing your socks."

Roma held down the twitch of his smile. He was trying to appear serious in front of the stranger, because Roma hated having a sense of humor in front of strangers, and Juliette made it her mission to provoke him intentionally.

"I'm so very sorry. We ought to have more work for you next time." He pulled her chair out too, then took the kettle from her hands and returned it to the stove. "We can't have you wasting that brain on socks."

In the years that they had been running their business—if an illegal weapons trading ring could be called a business—Juliette and Roma usually met with their contacts together, scampering out the door with a bag and piling into their car as if each drive out of the township was a big adventure. This time, however, there was a delivery coming from the city on the same day that they had a supplier wanting to meet, and so Juliette had stayed behind to make sure their stock was correct while Roma had driven out for the meeting. Roma was better at negotiations anyway, so she preferred it when he did the talking. According to one man whom they didn't work with anymore, Juliette was "scary" and "too easily prone to making threats."

He hadn't been *wrong*, per se, but that still wasn't very polite.

"Sock organizing wasn't so bad once I got the hang of it," Juliette said. "I didn't realize you had such big feet."

Roma choked on his tea. He scrambled to put his cup down before he spilled anything, coughing once to get the tea back into the right pipe. Juliette picked up her own cup innocently, taking a sip.

"You'll be glad to hear that I didn't have a particularly interesting time either," Roma said when he recovered. Fortunately for him, he had managed to play off the cough. "Until I was driving back and Yulun here dove in front of the car."

The boy, Yulun, perked up at the sound of his name. Now he knew he was being summoned into the conversation.

"Yes, I was wondering why you had picked up a stray." Juliette returned to speaking Chinese, extending a hand in Yulun's direction. They almost never brought anyone into their actual house, so this had to be something different from the usual clientele. "I'm Mrs. Mai."

Mai. The easiest combination of "Cai" and "Montagov," perhaps the least original method of creating an alias in the history of starting anew. Roma and Juliette had butted heads too much about whose name to begin with if they were to hyphenate . . . not because either wanted their own put first, but rather the other way around. Juliette wanted to be a Montagov; Roma insisted there was too much baggage attached. In her head, she still liked the sound of Juliette Montagova, because that was his name, and that was all that mattered. But it was better to use a Chinese name in Zhouzhuang, better for Roma to pass himself off as half-Chinese when his features ran close enough to be convincing, or else even more people might start getting suspicious about who they really were and what they had run from.

"Mai tàitài," Yulun greeted politely, shaking her hand. "I need your help. I assume you make the big calls. Please."

Juliette cast a glance over to Roma. "Did you hear that? He thinks I'm in charge."

"Don't pretend to be shocked." Roma's arm slid around the back of her chair. He yanked off one of the loose threads dangling from her dress—she had drastically toned down her wardrobe since fleeing Shanghai, but Juliette's version of toned-down still involved complex embroidery—then turned back to Yulun and said, "Tell her what you told me."

With some hesitance, Yulun shuffled forward in his seat. The chair leg scraped against the floorboards with a grating sound.

"I heard that you're the people to go to for weapons," he said. "I . . . I wanted to acquire some, but I don't have the means to meet the prices." He looked into his lap. "I was hoping that you might be open to an exchange of some sort. I'm great at running messages."

Juliette blinked, tilting her head curiously. A wisp of hair fell into her eyes. She attempted to blow it back, only her hair was long these days, growing far past her shoulders, so the huff did nothing except stick the lock to the side of her cheek.

"We're not really hiring right now," Juliette replied. She felt Roma trail a finger along her arm, the contact unhurried, more an instinct than something he was consciously aware of doing.

The silence drew out in the kitchen. Juliette shook her hair back into place. "But I do want to know why exactly you are trying to come into possession of weapons. You're not our usual demographic."

Yulun's gaze flickered over to Roma. He must have divulged this already, if Roma was willing to bring him all the way here to get Juliette's opinion.

"My fiancée is being threatened."

Ah. Juliette let out a small sigh, leaning into her chair. Of course it was something like this that got Roma's sympathy. Him and his soft heart. She adored him so much that it hurt.

"She's not from around here," Yulun went on. "She fled Vladivostok three years ago and entered Shanghai as a refugee before making her way farther inland."

He reached into his pocket and pulled out a picture. Clearly Roma hadn't seen this yet, because he leaned forward too and jolted immediately in surprise. His reaction was almost indiscernible, but he still had his hand against Juliette's arm, and she felt his tension like it was her own.

Yulun's fiancée looked just like Alisa, Roma's little sister.

The differences were evident enough that they were clearly two different people, and yet upon first glance Juliette would have easily made the mistake, from the blond curls to the deep-set dark eyes crinkled in a smile.

"I'm all she has," Yulun finished softly. "I was hoping you could help me. If not with weaponry, then . . ." The boy trailed off. When he slumped his shoulders, all his strength left him. "Someone from her past keeps contacting her. If weapons aren't an option, I had hoped you might sell your safeguarding."

Roma finally glanced away from the photo, one of his brows quirking up.

"You didn't mention that part on the drive." His tone had turned perplexed. "What sort of safeguarding could we possibly provide? We run a small business, not a security force."

Yulun gulped tightly. He reached into his pocket again and this time pulled out what appeared to be a newspaper clipping.

"You once offered protection, didn't you?" He unfolded the clipping slowly. The two portraits were revealed first, then the large-print headline above it:

Commemorating the Star-Crossed Lovers of Shanghai

Juliette Cai & Roma Montagov

1907–1927

"Juliette Cai and Roma Montagov, heir to the Scarlet Gang and heir to the White Flowers, the children of feuding families born into a bloody war, defying everything to end the cycle and be together." Yulun uttered each word with intention. As if he had heard those lines from elsewhere long ago and was reciting them from memory. "I had hoped that, of all people, you would understand."

The portrait sketches were uncannily accurate. Juliette picked up the newspaper clipping and held it to the afternoon light, looking for some sort of plausible deniability.

She found none. These were their faces, no doubt about it. Roma, however, didn't even glance at the portraits.

"You must be mistaken," he said. "I have never even heard the name Roma Montagov before. City gossip doesn't make its way to Zhouzhuang."

"What?" Yulun exclaimed, taken aback. "But you were *just* speaking Russian."

"Was I? I can't remember."

Yulun turned to Juliette next, his mouth opening and closing in incredulity. He pointed behind her. "You have a painting back there of Shanghai's wàitān."

Juliette craned over her shoulder, squinting at the frame and acting like she had never realized what it contained. Her cousin, Celia, bought it for her after Juliette admitted she was starting to forget the Bund—the ocean salt smell, the creaking boardwalk under her feet. Shanghai was a coastal city, an open port that pulsated with constant activity, ships arriving without pause and movement tearing through its streets at such speed that the city delivered its highest highs in the same breath as its lowest lows. Zhouzhuang was the exact opposite. It held the promise of haven in its stillness, protective layers formed in every direction with the leisurely speed at which its waters flowed.

"What a neat coincidence," she said, playing along with the bluff that Roma had started. "We hail from Harbin, though, not Shanghai."

Slowly Juliette pushed the newspaper clipping back toward Yulun. He didn't look like he believed her, but how could he possibly prove that they were lying, short of accusing them outright?

"If I'm reading this correctly, these people are long dead," she said gently. "Here." Pitying the boy, Juliette grabbed a pen from the counter behind her and quickly wrote a number on the paper edge: the communal telephone line in the township. "Give us a call for proper business when you have the means. But we're not the ones you're looking for. I'm sorry."

Her apology was sincere. She had once believed that inheriting the Scarlet Gang would give her immense power, that she would be able to help the people who needed it and stomp down the people trying to hurt her. But that kind of power was never supposed to be concentrated in one place, and a position like that would only draw up an unending list of enemies trying to cause her harm. She preferred a life free from the Scarlet Gang to a magnitude that was beyond words, and yet there was always going to be the little pang in her heart when she couldn't make things happen with a snap of her finger anymore.

Yulun took the newspaper clipping, returning it to his pocket alongside the photo of his fiancée. His lower lip wobbled. Before it could happen again, he steadied his expression, giving an accepting nod.

Roma stood and circled around the table. "I will walk you out," he said, clapping his hand down on Yulun's shoulder. "Are you able to get yourself back home?"

Yulun stood as well, looking dejected. "Yes, don't worry about me. I'm sorry to be a bother."

"Ah, we don't mind being enlivened once in a while." They disappeared into the living room, the murmur of conversation carrying on for a few more minutes before the front door opened and closed.

Juliette sighed, propping her elbows onto the table and resting her chin in her hands. She was still holding that pose when Roma returned to the kitchen, her eyes flicking up and latching onto him. He leaned against the archway, raising a brow as if to ask why she was staring, but she didn't look away. She liked admiring him without being afraid of getting caught. She liked it when she spotted him at the open market unexpectedly, breaking into a run and surprise-attacking him from the back, getting a laugh in response instead of a gun pulled on her. Their past had made every moment of their future a novelty, and she would never get sick of peppering him with kisses when she woke him up in the mornings, waiting for him to draw away before she was willing to stop—only he always refused to draw away first, offering his face with the biggest grin.

She would have thought that the addictive thrill would wear off after the first year. Perhaps once they started getting used to living without fear, living without the weight of two families and a whole city on their shoulders. But the truth was that weight would never fully fade, so neither did the knowledge that they had achieved something unbelievable in finding peace. Sometimes Juliette still jumped if a restaurant owner dropped a metal bowl on the ground, convinced that there were gunshots in the distance and she needed to go break up a fight between gangsters. Even if she realized quickly that there was nothing to be afraid of, her thoughts would be foggy and her palms clammy all day long, unsettling her stomach until she managed to distract herself. Sometimes Roma still woke up panicked in the middle of the night, shouting Juliette's name as if she had been pulled away in his dream, and though Juliette would be right beside him, her hands clasping his face, whispering, "I'm here, I'm right here, my love, it's okay," his heart wouldn't stop thudding under her touch until morning, neither of them sleeping.

Juliette got out of her chair and walked toward him now. Put her arms around his neck without saying anything, letting him draw her closer until they were pressed flush.

"I'm sorry," Roma murmured. "If I had known he was going to spring that on us, I wouldn't have bothered."

"No, I'm happy you wanted to see if we could help," Juliette replied. She searched his gaze, trying to communicate how deeply she meant it. The very fact that he could afford to be kind, that they could try to be ordinary people extending a hand wherever possible, was a beautiful thing. It was only unfortunate that the boy had such high expectations, and Roma and Juliette could hardly meet them without exposing too much of themselves.

It had taken a tremendous amount of coordination to make use of every old contact they had in Shanghai without giving away their identities. Some contacts required blackmailing before they were willing to cooperate; others required a very roundabout series of white lies to convince them that they had been plugged into this trading ring all along. Either way, the information that Roma and Juliette clutched individually was worth its weight in gold when put together, and there was no denying the power of their pasts each time they reached out to reinforce a connection. While a few seemed to suspect some leak in the former innermost gang circles, no one would guess it was Roma and Juliette resurrected from the dead. So long as the ones who got close enough to see their faces didn't start spreading rumors, it was a fine setup. Preservation of their identities was always going to be the highest priority. They hadn't worked so hard for this new life only for it to shatter.

Juliette did feel bad about it, though. About lying to the boy. About lying to those she had abandoned in Shanghai. She knew it haunted Roma, too, leaving his sister in the city. It was too dangerous to risk Alisa coming in and out if she knew that they were located here, and they had been waiting and waiting for the political upheaval in the city to lessen before making contact. Juliette wouldn't even have told Celia if her cousin hadn't been the one to smuggle them out here.

The years were wearing on. They were children growing into adult faces, waiting for a moment of contentment that might never come. She lived every day aware that Celia might get caught as a Communist agent while traveling into Zhouzhuang, that she would be hauled in by the current government and accused of protecting criminals who should have been reformed in Juliette's case and executed in Roma's. She was glad that her hand had been forced, achingly glad that she saw her cousin almost once a month, whenever Celia had time to visit, but Juliette would have accepted the burden of playing dead if it meant safety for those she loved most. She and Roma were the same that way. It was their greatest flaw and their greatest strength at once, and she doubted that would ever change.

Maybe if Yulun called again, though, Juliette would slide a

handgun his way. Free of charge, and when Roma was looking in the other direction.

As if he could hear her frantic internal squall, Roma brushed his lips against her temple, quieting every thought.

"Well," he said, "I'm always happy to make you happy."

Juliette beamed. She couldn't help it. As much as she thought of herself as hardened steel, Roma turned her lovesick at a speed that verged on embarrassing. They had been together for four years now—together properly, not counting their terrible on-off phases, or else they would soon be approaching nine—and loving him was still so *easy*, despite being removed from everything they once knew. All it took was her heart on her sleeve and his pulled open too, and she was constantly tickled pink by her favorite person.

"Also . . ."

Just as Juliette was about to pull away, returning her arms to her sides, Roma grabbed her jaw, stopping her from further movement. Though the move was made with the pretense of being daunting, Roma and Juliette had *actually* tried to kill each other a few times in those off phases—some of the instances coming quite close—so the feigned rough handling only made Juliette grin.

"'I didn't realize you had such big feet'?" Roma mimicked. "Dorogaya, I'm shocked and disappointed."

"At my terrible housekeeping?"

"No, that you have such poor observation skills." He grabbed her by the waist suddenly and threw her over his shoulder. All of Juliette's loose hair fell into her eyes as she turned upside down with a squeal, clutching onto the hem of Roma's shirt for some semblance of balance while he walked them into the bedroom. "I guess I'll just have to show you again so you are certain next time."

2

oma was a late riser by nature. He hadn't realized this
tidbit about himself for the first nineteen years of his life,
when he would jump out of bed at the hint of dawn, frantically sorting through the day's problems before they could arise.
Time had never belonged to him back when he was the heir to the
White Flowers; time belonged to whatever the city's next task was,
spurring him to run to the loudest call.

These days, he either let Juliette wake him—*she* was an early
riser by nature—or he stirred back into the world once he felt well
rested enough, stretching his arms upon the sheets, half of him
buried in the mass of pillows that took up most of their bed.

Roma lifted his head blearily, trying to listen for Juliette in the
house. It was quiet. When he turned over and rubbed his eyes,
the metal of his wedding ring cool against his cheek, there was a
note atop the small table at his side, written in tiny English letters
that he needed to squint to read.

> *I took your shirt hostage. The ransom is three kisses.*
> *Pay up or the whole wardrobe gets it.*
> ♥ *J*

Roma laughed under his breath, rolling out of the blankets and
grabbing the trousers that she had been so kind as to not also take

hostage. Mornings in late September meant that there was the slightest chill in the air when he opened the bedroom door, but he still padded into the washroom without finding a second shirt, taking his time brushing his teeth and flattening his hair. He knew where Juliette would be waiting. They had adopted a regular weekday routine, and these early hours were for whatever entertained them the most, because the real work and meetings didn't start until noon, when their suppliers started driving into the township to bring stock and their hired help came around with equipment and messages and whatever else the business needed.

"Has anyone ever told you," Roma began, opening the front door, "that you leave threats like a gangster heiress?"

"Never heard that once in my life," Juliette replied without missing a beat. She turned over her shoulder to look at him, perched at the canal with her legs dangling over the edge. A ray of sunlight lit her frame in a perfect rectangular block, putting a gleam in her eye and a redness to her lips that he wanted to consume whole. It didn't matter that he had kissed her until they were both delirious last night. It didn't matter that he had her forever and ever to kiss, past death and into whatever afterlife existed. He still couldn't get enough of her.

Juliette's eyes dipped delightedly to his chest, then back up again, grinning like she could tell what he was thinking. She probably could. She'd probably thrown on his shirt over her pajama shorts knowing exactly what it would do to him to see her like this, the sleeves slightly too long and the collar askew, the dip of her clavicle more visible than it had any right to be.

With an exaggerated sound of effort, Roma dropped himself down beside his wife, forcing a frown.

"I only came outside to get my shirt back. You've left me shivering like a sad little ragamuffin."

A breeze blew along the canal as if to emphasize his point,

rustling the weeping willow tree to their right. The leaves looked like translucent fairy wings, every shade of green as bright as emeralds. Though the waters always gave their surroundings a bite, the sun was warm on his bare shoulders.

"Pay the ransom, then."

"You'll make it that easy for me? No further extortion?"

Juliette leaned forward, her eyes crinkling. "Maybe I won't give it back after the payment. Start counting up to three, and I guess we'll see."

Science could tell him that the ground was below his feet and the sky was above his head and the early light of day was upon his back. Roma wouldn't listen. To him, Juliette was the sun.

He closed the space between them, eyes shutting a heartbeat before their lips made contact. It was second nature to him, a function easier than breathing. She was made for him, and he for her; his inhales were finished by her exhales, their motions anticipated by the other even if it was something as mundane as Roma lifting his hand for the dishcloth and Juliette sliding it his way before he had spoken aloud.

Roma cupped her neck, his fingers brushing the smooth locks of her hair out of the way before sinking down to her collar.

"One," he murmured against her mouth, undoing the top button and beginning his mission to get his shirt back. "Two." Their lips brushed again, the contact luxuriously slow. The next button snapped open. Juliette made a noise at the back of her throat that sent his every nerve ending into overdrive.

"Three—"

"*Stop making babies on the front stoop!*"

Juliette tore away, so startled by the voice calling across the canal that she would have tipped right into the water if Roma hadn't recovered quicker and clutched her elbow to right her. Succeeding in frightening them, their old neighbor—Mrs. Fan—gave a great big cackle, propping her bucket higher on her hip and turning the corner to go around to the front of her house. She had walked out from her back door, which was directly connected to a set of stone steps that led down to the canal for laundry.

"Tā mā de—not cool, Fan nǎinai!" Juliette shouted after her.

"*Sorry, sorry, get back to it! I've been waiting for more kids around here, so I guess it's fine even if you make it a public activity. . . .*"

Her voice faded off as she got too distant to hear. Juliette huffed.

"It was *not* a public activity. There aren't even any windows facing us."

Roma resisted the urge to laugh when he knew it would only make her madder. In the first few months after they had settled in Zhouzhuang, the townspeople had been much colder toward them. Rightfully so, since no one knew where Roma and Juliette had suddenly popped up from. Then Juliette started bringing fish to the doors of every old woman along the main canals, and Roma would braid flower crowns for the children who played by the largest stone bridges. Though the townspeople still suspected that the two must have fled from something unlawful, they had come to treat Roma and Juliette like their own.

"I suppose that was our own fault. Come on, we're going to catch a cold."

Roma led them inside, giving up on getting his shirt back as he fetched a new one from the closet. It was hers now if she wanted it; he could afford to buy another in the exact same shape and color. Though they had started trading weapons as the avenue they knew best, it also happened to be a lucrative business, bringing in enough that they would often reject clients if they didn't like what the weapons were being used for.

"Breakfast?" Juliette asked, emerging from the bedroom while pinning her hair back. She had put on her own clothes: a qipao, light green with a flower stitched onto the shoulder.

Roma was already grabbing the coins on the living room desk, half his jacket dangling off his shoulder. "I'll race you."

"Stop it," Juliette threatened immediately. "Don't think I won't tackle you to the ground!"

As much as he would have loved a full-body tackle—because Juliette refused to admit that he could and would easily snatch her out of the air—he did slow by the door, sticking his arm into his sleeve properly and taking her hand when she walked out with him.

"Hey," she said. Her tone had changed, playful Juliette swapping out for serious Juliette. "I forgot to ask. . . . That picture yesterday looked familiar to you too, didn't it?"

He knew immediately what she meant. It would have been very difficult to miss the resemblance.

"It did," he answered softly.

Alisa was going to be turning eighteen this December. While he kept himself very informed on her life, he hadn't seen her properly in years, didn't know how his sister was faring past the news that Celia brought in. He and Juliette couldn't set foot back in Shanghai; it was far too easy to get caught if they showed their faces. Though he trusted Celia to watch after Alisa, perhaps trusted her even more than he was capable of trusting himself, he missed that mischief-maker crawling in and out of the cupboards while he was trying to have private conversations, missed her so much that the feeling latched onto him like a tumor. He and Juliette had survived in the literal sense, had built something precious in the wake of burning a hate-filled cycle into ash, but the people in Shanghai weren't wrong when they whispered about Roma Montagov and Juliette Cai being dead—they could never go back, and that had killed a huge part of what made them *them*.

Juliette squeezed his hand. They proceeded into the main part of town, little pebbles scattering underfoot on the roughly paved ground.

"We'll be able to see her soon," she promised. "Celia thinks the government isn't paying attention to former White Flowers anymore. It's getting too chaotic internally. The danger will lessen. It has to."

"Logically, I know you're right." Roma exhaled, tilting his head up to watch a bird take flight from one of the curved roof tiles. "Yet I hate the thought of endangering her. She's happy working for the Communists. I don't want to make her choose us or them."

It would have been easier if Alisa were less stubborn, if she had just gone with Marshall and Benedikt to Moscow, because Roma had contacted his two best friends within days of them settling there, out of the Nationalists' reach, and Benedikt had yelled at him so thoroughly for faking his death—*REALLY, ROMA?! THIS IS THE LAST AND FINAL TIME ANYONE DOES THIS, DO YOU UNDERSTAND ME?! GET YOUR WIFE ON THE LINE, I HAVE SOME WORDS FOR HER, TOO*—that he thought the international telephone audio might short out.

Juliette went to pay for vegetable buns. Roma waited while she bantered with the old man behind the shop counter, staring off into the distance. When Juliette brushed up against him again, handing over a small bag, he asked, "What if, by the time we contact her, she hates me for having kept away?"

"My love," Juliette chided immediately. "This is Alisa we are talking about." She bit into her bun. "She will only be happy to see you again. She's not as dramatic as I am."

At that, Roma's mouth twitched, recalling each time in the past he had kept away from Juliette and withheld information. He'd never do it now—not when their new lives depended on communicating as one functional unit—but at the time, he *had* believed he was making the best choice. He had only wanted to keep her safe.

"Besides," Juliette continued, "you pay her bills. I wouldn't be surprised if she has long figured it out."

That was also true. Roma was hardly subtle. He took a bite of the bun. Maybe the trick was to keep dropping larger and larger hints until Alisa figured out the truth, but not making contact so she didn't find them until it was safe to do so. Then again, he wouldn't put it past Alisa to somehow track them down anyway.

"Mr. Mai! Phone call!"

Roma whirled around, searching for whoever was shouting at him. On the other side of the main canal, one of the ladies who ran a tailoring business waved him over, gesturing to the communal phone line that was set up right outside her shop.

"Are we expecting anyone?" Juliette asked, sounding perplexed.

"Not until Ah Cao in the afternoon."

They made their way over to the telephone, crossing the stone bridge in a hurry. Juliette sidled right up to the wall as Roma picked up the receiver that had been left beside the hook for him, pressing it to his ear.

"Wéi?"

He heard a sharp, struggling intake of breath. Then: "It's . . . it's . . ."

Confused, Roma cast a look to Juliette, trying to signal that he couldn't hear anything. "I'm sorry, I can't—"

"It's Yulun," the voice finally managed in a quick breath. Over the line, Yulun continued heaving and sniffling, as if he were crying.

Roma switched from confused to concerned. "Is everything all right? Are you safe?"

Juliette leaned in close, putting her ear on the other side of the receiver in an attempt to listen in. They heard a few seconds more of sniffles, before:

"Please," Yulun sobbed. "She's going to be next. They're all dead."

3

Juliette closed her car door, surveying their surroundings. They had driven one township up, rumbling along the rural gravel to get to Yulun's location. Unlike Zhouzhuang, which was situated beside the tendrils of a colossal lake, this township lay deeper inland. There were no water passages, but it was still built in the older traditional style, albeit with thin cobblestoned paths weaving through the buildings in place of canals. Wide roads were reserved for proper towns and cities; here, Roma was forced to park by the township gate, blocked from proceeding any farther on a motor vehicle.

A cold breeze blew into their faces. Overhead, a clump of gray storm clouds had gathered densely, sending down a faint rumble of thunder.

"We need to talk about your driving," Juliette remarked. She circled around the front of the vehicle, her heels stepping awkwardly on the rough stone ground. "I thought we were about to crash multiple times."

"I'm sorry," Roma replied dryly. He lifted his arm, and Juliette ducked under, pressing close while they walked. "Personally, I think I drive quite well for someone who had chauffeurs all his life."

"Oooh, he had *chauffeurs*."

"Dorogaya, I know *you* are not making fun of me right now."

Juliette bit back her snort as the two of them entered the township.

They had set off immediately after Yulun's alarming phone call. He had barely been coherent in his attempt to explain what he meant, so Juliette had taken over the receiver to tell him to take a deep breath, give them his address, and put the phone down. . . . They were on their way to see what on earth was going on.

It was fortunately not too suspicious for Roma and Juliette to be visiting these neighboring townships. They had plenty of business here and plenty of contacts who would play along if a local resident asked who they were here to see. When Juliette peered around, however, the narrow streets were near empty. Not even an elderly shop owner out on the perch, hands behind their back and taking in the fresh air. There was *always* an elderly shop owner taking in the fresh air.

"Something doesn't seem right," Juliette muttered to Roma.

His arm, already over her shoulder, tightened around her. "Hear anything?"

"Not yet." They exchanged a glance. Silently, with only a nod passed between them, they agreed to be wary.

The address that Yulun had provided was deep in the township, number 280 on Liyi Street. They had already found Liyi Street—which was actually a long, squiggly pathway rather than a street per se—but they were only passing number 34. Juliette observed the mailboxes as they walked, the little green containers propped up on the exterior walls. Each door was closed firmly. Each shop front had pulled their gate down, shuttered and padlocked.

She didn't like this one bit. As quiet as Zhouzhuang was, the sense of solitude she treasured there came from its unhurried deliberateness: one boat bobbing down the canal, one tree overgrowing for years without pruning.

Yulun's township, on the other hand, felt haunted. It was an unnatural quiet instead of a peaceful quiet, as if every chattering neighbor had turned their backs on one another.

Somewhere around number 90, Juliette stopped to glance upward. A teahouse sat to her left, because if there was one thing that rural townships could be entrusted to have in abundance, it was teahouses. Its second level had an open structure, a balcony protruding from its main building to offer patrons their choice of seating in fresh air. A flash of movement receded from the balcony. All the tables were empty, but Juliette was pretty sure the owner was watching the street from above, hurrying back into the shadows as soon as Juliette looked.

"Anyone there?" she called up.

No response.

Roma pulled her hand to continue along Liyi Street. Another clap of low thunder rumbled from afar.

They passed bicycles chained outside residences, shopping baskets that had been stacked neatly on front stoops, discarded bags of roasted chestnut shells. At number 200, Juliette crouched beside a large ceramic pot, where a plant that resembled a miniature tree was growing. She pressed her finger to the soil. It was damp.

It wasn't that this township had cleared out. There were certainly people here, or at least someone who continued watering their plants out front.

"I see someone," Roma said suddenly.

Juliette immediately pulled her attention away from the plant. Some distance ahead, with the pathway curving downhill, a man stood in front of one of the doors, sifting through envelopes in his hand—the postman, gauging by his uniform and the bulging bag hanging from his shoulder.

"Let's go ask him where everyone is," Juliette suggested, already hurrying forward. Under usual circumstances, people who lived in these parts had no filter. They would tell state secrets if asked nicely enough.

She slowed her pace as she got nearer, feigning nonchalance.

Close on her tail, Roma put his hands in his pockets, mimicking her casual air. The postman in front of number 213 didn't look familiar, so his work territory probably didn't extend over to Zhouzhuang. Still, Juliette greeted him as if he were an old friend, and the postman turned to her happily, tipping his hat.

She took the opportunity to stop.

"I hope I'm not interrupting," she said, "but do you usually deliver around here?"

"I absolutely do," the postman replied. A tag on his uniform gave his surname as Liao. Under his cap, his hair was entirely white. He seemed to give Juliette and Roma a closer appraisal before asking: "The two of you come in from the city?"

"No," Roma answered immediately. "Only from Zhouzhuang. We're visiting family."

"We think they might have gone elsewhere for the week, because no one was home when we knocked," Juliette added.

"It's as empty as the new year, isn't it?" Mr. Liao agreed.

Terribly so. Juliette might have been inclined to believe a holiday had turned the whole place hush, if only it weren't months away from the new year. Besides, that would usually clear out the cities and larger towns where civilians immigrated to work, not the smaller townships. The new year made these parts louder and livelier than ever, if anything, because everyone in the city came home to their rural origins.

"Rather strange," Juliette commented. "What's the cause?"

Mr. Liao immediately looked over his shoulder. He scanned their premises thoroughly before turning back.

"I don't live here, so I wasn't certain either until I heard from Mrs. Chang on Tianneng Street. Lots of foreign men lurking around the area. They claim to be searching for someone and want to make no trouble, but anyone who runs into them is questioned aggressively." The postman sifted through his envelopes as he spoke, trying to find what he was delivering next. "Mrs. Chang was followed all the way home. Said they banged on her door for half an hour when she couldn't give an answer."

Juliette grimaced. At her side, Roma looked uneasy as well. Yulun had mentioned his fiancée being threatened. He also said she had fled from Vladivostok, which was on the easternmost coast of the Soviet Union. This could be the threat Yulun was talking about.

"When you say foreign men . . . ," Juliette clarified anyway. "Western foreign or Russian foreign?"

Mr. Liao shrugged. "Could be Russian. Apparently they speak běndì huà fine, so that's my guess."

"I suppose we ought to clear out soon too." Roma nudged her with his elbow. Juliette nudged him back. "Thank you."

With another tip of his hat, the postman turned back to his giant bag of letters.

"What do you think?" Juliette whispered when they were some distance away. "Is this enough to get Yulun that worked up on the phone?"

Roma shook his head. "Something worse must have happened."

A few men causing trouble was nothing to scoff at, but it certainly wasn't overly dire, either. The residents in this township seemed to have decided to keep their heads down and wait out the days until the men got fed up with making trouble. This whole country had been under warlord rule for years before the current government took over. People were used to closing their doors tightly when men were strong-arming their way through the streets.

As they approached number 280, Juliette pressed on the sheath at her leg to make sure her weapons were secure. It wasn't that she expected to find danger, but it would always do well to be prepared.

"Number 280," Roma said aloud. They stopped, observing the house.

It looked like every other building down the pathway, two

stories high and painted modestly in brown. Though Juliette had intended to knock on the front door as soon as she stepped close, she had scarcely lifted her hand before there was a loud *thud* from inside.

She and Roma veered back.

"Yulun?" Roma called. He slapped his palm flat against the door, making sure his knock carried loudly. "Are you in there?"

Yulun didn't answer. There was only more strange rustling.

"I don't want to be overly alarmist," Juliette said, her pulse picking up, "but it sounds like there's a struggle going on inside."

She tried the front handle. It wouldn't budge. The door looked too sturdy to kick down. While Roma kept knocking, Juliette hurried over to the window, cupping her hands to the glass so she could peer inside. As was the case with most rural residences, the house had low ceilings, so despite the two floors, it still hovered at a modest height before the roof tiles started to curve up. Its structure was narrow, though. The first floor was a living space, so the second floor had to be a bedroom. There was little room for anything else.

"Roma," she said. With a wince of effort, Juliette pushed the heavy window glass up. "Give me a boost, would you?"

At times like these, she really missed her American dresses. She might have been able to pull herself through if her qipao fabric didn't press so tightly around her hips. Fortunately, Roma was quick to grab her waist and lift her to the ledge, letting her swivel on the window and pull her legs in before hopping into the house.

The back door was wide open. Juliette scanned the living room, then immediately shot her gaze up the stairs, where she heard the barest grunt of movement.

Roma climbed in through the small window frame too, landing on the wooden floorboards firmly.

"Cover me."

Roma shifted instantly, surveying the back door while Juliette charged up the stairs. "Be careful."

Juliette's response was to draw a weapon. She took the stairs two at a time, teeth gritted hard and heart pounding against her ribs. At once, she rounded the top of the stairs to find Yulun lying motionless at the foot of a bed and a girl pinned to the floor a few paces away, struggling against a tall man with a cloth in his hand.

"Hey!" Juliette shouted.

The girl's head jerked left, seeking the sound with a frantic, heaving gasp.

"Help!" she screamed in Russian. "*Please!*"

The man lurched forward, intending to clamp the cloth around her mouth. Just before he could make contact, however, he craned back to avoid the girl's flailing arms, exposing his neck.

Juliette knew how to take an opening. Without missing a beat, she threw her knife, landing it dead center in the man's throat.

4

"Oh my—"

Roma skidded to a stop at the top of the stairs, coming up behind Juliette and taking in the scene. He squeezed her shoulder first, hovering for a beat until she touched the back of his hand lightly in assurance, before rushing to Yulun's side.

The boy's chest moved with his shallow inhale-exhale. *Thank God.* Not dead, only knocked out. Roma tapped Yulun's face, but the boy gave no response. There was a rather intense red bruise freshly marked on his temple. Roma winced. He had been knocked in the head like that one too many times and, from unfortunate personal experience, he knew how terrible it was to wake up afterward. It would be no good to rush him.

Juliette went to help the girl, her shoes clacking on the floor in her hurry. Roma glanced over just as she was nudging aside the dead man with her heel. She extended a hand down.

"Are there any more of them nearby?"

They had just been hearing about possible Russian men on the streets looking for Yulun's fiancée, but this man lying dead on the floor was Chinese. On the side of his neck, right beside the entry point of Juliette's blade, he had a tattoo of an angel.

"I—I don't think so," the girl answered hesitantly. She took the helping hand, her shoulders pulled small when she straightened to her feet. "Thank you. You saved me."

Juliette shrugged. She always got a little embarrassed when receiving gratitude, though she hid it well with a self-assured attitude. Only Roma knew how to spot that flush of pink at the tip of her nose, then that twitch in her hand when she bent down to tug her knife out of the man's throat, sending a spray of blood across her ankles.

In unison, Roma and the girl winced. While Roma continued watching his wife to make sure she was okay, the girl hurried over to Yulun, gingerly touching his forehead.

"He will come to in a little while," Roma assured her. "There is no immediate danger from his injuries."

The girl nodded. Her picture truly hadn't lied: when a strand of hair fell into her face, Roma couldn't comprehend how uncanny her resemblance to Alisa was. Though the dark blond color served as the most obvious point of comparison, her curls fell from her head in the exact same way too, from the tight, unruly locks that stayed messy at the top to the looser waves along her back. She was pale as she brushed the strand away.

"What happened?" Juliette asked from across the room. She knew she needed to jump in. Roma was practically at a loss for words while he flailed over the incomprehensible illusion of his little sister crouching in front of him.

"They have been threatening me for some time. I suppose it is only now that they finally found my location and . . ." The girl hesitated, trailing off midsentence. "How much has Yulun told you?"

Juliette didn't entirely answer the question either. "I gather that you know he came to us for help."

A nod. "I could hardly believe him, but he said you were . . . well . . ."

"Devochka, what's your name?" Roma interrupted, before she could go waving *their* names around and they would have to continue telling blatant lies. "Pardon us for not asking sooner."

The girl looked down, pressing her hand to Yulun's cheek. "That's all right. There was a lot going on."

On cue, from where she stood, Juliette shook free a bedsheet she had rummaged out from one of the cabinet drawers and draped it over the dead body. She met Roma's eyes.

You're helping me drag him out afterward, she mouthed in English. Dear Lord.

"I am Milyena," the girl, meanwhile, was saying. "You can call me Mila. Everyone around here does."

"Very well, Mila." Roma braced his hands on his knees and stood up, wincing from the fast movement. "See if you can assist Yulun upright. My wife will help you get him into our car."

Mila blinked. "Car?"

"You cannot possibly stay here if your location has been exposed," Juliette added. "It is only a short drive, I promise. Now . . ." Juliette looked to Roma again, inclining her head toward the covered corpse. "Use your strong muscles for me, please, qīn'ài de?"

Rather unceremoniously, Roma dumped the attacker's body into a canal.

"This is terrible," he grumbled under his breath, dusting his hands off. "The poor fish."

"The poor fish?" Juliette echoed. "We're feeding the fish so many good nutrients. This is going to be the best meal they've had in years. Delicious human meat."

If he didn't love Juliette so much, he would really spend every waking moment in fear of what went on in that mind of hers. But because he loved her, and he was clearly out of his mind too, he only turned and steered her back into the house. After returning to Zhouzhuang, the priority had been getting Yulun out of the car and giving Mila a blanket so she would stop shaking. Only then did

Roma and Juliette come back to the car and heave the dead body out of the trunk—well, Roma heaved and Juliette issued instructions while lugging merely one ankle. Roma was very certain that Juliette herself possessed the strength to be throwing dead bodies into canals, but she always liked pleading weakness. Perhaps she just preferred watching him sweat instead.

When they entered the house again, Yulun was awake. They had set him on the sofa, with Juliette fretting the whole time about the material fraying at the sides and pressing uncomfortably if Yulun put his head down. Roma had voiced his doubt that Yulun would mind being scratched by the sofa, but Juliette had hurried for a pillow nonetheless, and now Yulun was looking confusedly at the green cushion beside him, cross-stitched with the top half of a frog.

Juliette didn't have the patience for cross-stitching. She had learned that rather late into her project. Not that it had stopped her from keeping her half-completed frog around anyway.

"So," she said, her voice carrying as she wandered into the adjoining kitchen. She had left the kettle on the stove to boil. "Start from the beginning."

"The beginning of the attack?" Yulun asked.

"Or the beginning of everything?" Mila continued softly.

Roma leaned against the wall, widening his eyes at Juliette for the briefest second when she turned around holding the kettle. That had been a little eerie. Maybe this was how people felt when he and Juliette spoke in accidental unison.

"The beginning of everything, of course," Roma said. He hesitated a moment, then added in Russian, "You can switch if you want. We will understand."

Mila pulled the blanket closer to her shoulders. Her Chinese was accented, words coming slowly while she considered what she wanted to say, so there was no doubt it would be easier to explain in her native tongue. But she shook her head. She patted Yulun's arm, indicating that she wanted him to be following along too, and he wouldn't if she switched.

"The beginning," Mila said. She fiddled with the corner of the blanket. "It is a commonplace story, I suppose. I am an orphan from a small town you have never heard about. Life was hard. Work doing menial labor was harder. After I turned fourteen, I was starting to scratch into the last of the savings that my mother had left me, and I needed to find some way to earn more or risk starving to death. Then one day . . . well, it was like some sign from the heavens when I saw an advertisement seeking paid volunteers for an experiment."

An experiment. Roma supposed this was where the story stopped being commonplace. He nodded his gratitude when Juliette came back into the living room, giving him a steaming teacup and setting three more cups down on the table.

"I followed the posting to a facility in Vladivostok. It seemed perfectly ordinary. The facility hosted five of us, all girls my age. They gave us communal housing. Food at regular hours. They even gave us nicer clothes because the ones we came in with were getting shabby."

"Who is *they*?" Juliette asked, sitting next to Mila. Roma took a sip of tea.

Mila hesitated. "That depends, I suppose," she decided. "There was a board of men in charge of the overall operation who would come into the facility every once in a while. But we interacted the most with two scientists who lived with us at the facility. A young man who only went by Mr. Pyotr and an elderly man named Lourens Van Dijk."

Roma spat out his tea. At least he was still holding the cup, so it occurred in a dignified manner, all the water caught neatly. Judging by the way Juliette pressed her hand to her mouth to hide her upturned lips, though, he gathered that she thought otherwise.

"What?" Yulun asked, eyes growing wide. "Why did you react like that?"

"Lourens"—Roma coughed to regain his composure, setting the cup on the fireplace mantel—"is an old friend of ours."

"Speak for yourself. . . ." Juliette smoothed away her amusement, her hands tucking under her arms instead. "That nutty scientist only ever gave me headaches. And a slice of orange."

"He—" Roma frowned. "I remember the orange slice, but why did he give you headaches?"

"Do you forget? His work in the labs persistently messed up Scarlet supply. You stole our products and changed them nearly every month."

Yulun suddenly straightened up, clutching onto this first bit of concrete evidence that he had been correct about their identities. Still, Juliette's claim was rather inaccurate, so Roma couldn't resist arguing: "But that wasn't Lourens's fault. That was mine."

"Yes, correct. *You* also gave me headaches. Frequently."

Roma winced. There was nothing more he could say to that in his defense. Indeed, he used to make himself a thorn in Juliette's side frequently, if only because the city had forced them apart and it was better to get her hatred than nothing at all. These days, though he didn't need to resort to being a menace anymore, he still liked rolling onto her side of the bed when she was ignoring him for a book and receiving the honor of being smacked away with her pillow.

Roma turned back to Mila. "So you mean to say they experimented on you?"

"It was nothing horrific," Mila replied carefully. "We took medication. They measured our vitals every day. The facility said they were only interested in health-care advancements."

On the sofa, Juliette had started chewing on her bottom lip, her fingers tapping on her cup. If her head had gone to the same place as Roma's, they were both thinking about the last time they had heard news about Lourens: when Celia had visited and warned that Rosalind, Juliette's cousin and Celia's sister, wasn't the same anymore, that she had gotten sick and Lourens had saved her with some sort of advanced science before disappearing off the face of the earth. That had to have been before he went to Vladivostok.

"We realized something was wrong the first time we heard the two arguing. Mr. Pyotr and Lourens, that is. They hadn't closed the door to the office, and Dasha waved us over to listen. The new round of experimentation wasn't ready yet, but the previous day Mr. Pyotr had injected us anyway. Lourens wasn't happy."

A light prickle of cold sweat moved down Roma's neck. Yulun reached for Mila's hand.

"We shook it off. Believed everything was fine. Our lives in that facility were wonderfully content, and for a group of girls with nothing else, no one wanted it ruined." Mila sighed. "But that did not last long. I started to lose long swaths of time. I would look out the window and not remember when it had turned to evening. I would sit inside a room and struggle to recall when I had walked in. The undeniable moment came when I woke up one night and found Dasha missing from her bed. I waited for hours before she returned to the facility, and she claimed she hadn't gone anywhere. Even though I watched her come in through the front entrance."

"They didn't lock you in or anything, then," Juliette clarified. "You were free to come and go as you pleased?"

"Of course." Mila's brow scrunched, as if she couldn't possibly imagine a scenario where they held her in captivity. "That was what made it so easy to flee eventually. I kept asking about Dasha and what was wrong with her. Mr. Pyotr kept insisting it was a measly side effect that would go away soon. It would have been easy to take his word for it if Lourens hadn't left that next week.

He tried to tell me something at the door, but Mr. Pyotr forced him to go before he could get a word out. Lourens never came back. I wouldn't be surprised if he's in hiding from the board now too."

For a moment, Mila fell into silence, smoothing her hair down by rapidly pulling at the strands beside her face. Had Lourens seen the resemblance too when she did that? Had he felt the guilt creep in, remembering Alisa darting in and out of the labs whenever she was on the search for her big brother?

"The board started coming more often to talk behind closed doors. We got more adamant. We demanded answers. And one night, when the five of us crowded Mr. Pyotr to make a ruckus, he shouted for us to *stop*, and we did. It felt like some invisible hand was holding me still, like he could say anything in that moment and I would have to follow instruction."

Goddammit, Lourens, Roma thought. Always inventing new science, for better or for worse.

"How can that be *allowed?*" Mila asked, and her voice cracked. "How could I stay there knowing that at any moment he could bid me to do whatever he wanted? We all fled on the first ship out, separating once we got to Shanghai. Valentina and Viktoria stayed in the city. Dasha and Lilya came inland with me, then said good-bye and proceeded farther when I wanted to stay in the quieter parts."

"How long ago was that?" Juliette asked quietly. Her eyes lifted, seeking Roma, communicating what she was thinking.

"Almost three years ago," Yulun answered on Mila's behalf. "December 1928."

"Yulun's mother owned the teahouse where I started working." The ghost of a smile appeared on Mila's lips. "I would have struggled greatly had I not met him that first day there."

Which meant she had been left in peace for so long. She had been settled for almost as much time as Roma and Juliette had been leading their new life too. When Juliette broke eye contact, visible pain flitted across her expression in empathy. Roma felt the same pang twist his stomach.

"So why now?" he asked. "Why not come after you when you escaped?"

Mila gave a weak shrug.

"My speculations don't make any sense either. All I know is that, about a month ago, a letter showed up for me in Mr. Pyotr's handwriting. He said he wanted to help me, and there would be consequences if I didn't accept."

"I burned it, by the way," Yulun cut in. "Threw it right in the fire."

Mila cast him an amused look. It faded quickly as she continued her story. "He had found me, so it wasn't safe anymore if he could show up at any moment. We fled into the next town over. Except another letter showed up. We fled again."

"Let me guess," Juliette said. "The letters kept showing up."

Mila reached into her skirt pocket. "I kept this last one on me. It is probably the most concerning of them all."

Roma leaned in, grimacing when he took the slip of paper to read the words.

They are coming.

"Did this come postmarked?" he asked. "Any clue as to where it might have originated from?"

"They arrive in a blank envelope each time," Yulun answered. "I have half a mind to believe that Mr. Pyotr is dropping them off himself."

Which was . . . frightening. Juliette glanced over with her brow furrowed. Roma returned her feeling of disconcertment.

"That was four days ago," Mila said, gesturing to the warning. "The very same afternoon"—she took a deep, stuttering breath—

"I saw news of Valentina and Viktoria reported in the papers. Murdered, one day after the other." She paused. Squeezed her eyes shut, then opened them again, her voice steadying. "The papers didn't give names, but I know it was them. They worked as show-girls at different dance halls."

Roma put the slip of paper down on the table.

"The other two are dead too, aren't they?" he asked.

"Dasha and Lilya lived next door to each other in a township right outside Suzhou's borders, an hour's drive from here," Mila answered quietly. "Yulun went to go warn them this morning."

Yulun pinched the bridge of his nose, looking exhausted. "Dasha wasn't there," he supplied. "Though there was a bloody trail going into the alley. Lilya . . . Lilya was already cold. There was blood everywhere around her neck. I took one look and bolted."

Chances were, someone would find Dasha's body in the next few days. It would be foolish to hope otherwise.

"And that was when you called us," Roma concluded.

"I didn't know what else to do." Yulun's expression crumpled. "I really thought that staying in these rural areas would make it harder to find Mila. I thought it would keep her safe."

The living room fell into a hush. The scent of despair hung heavy, and when Juliette stood up abruptly, she waved her arms around as if she were trying to clear the smell out.

"Okay, here's the plan," she said. "I'm going to give you some knives, and then you and Mila are going to learn to defend your-selves in case another threat comes soon. Let's just hope we can get to the bottom of this *before* anything more arrives."

Juliette strode across the living room, her fists clenched and her shoulders tight. All of a sudden, Yulun stood as well, calling, "Wait!"

Juliette paused, one foot already in the hallway.

"I . . . I *was* right, no?" he said. "You're Juliette Cai."

"I'm not Juliette Cai."

Yulun furrowed his brow in sheer disbelief. "You cannot possibly still say that when—"

"It's Juliette Montagova." She lifted her hand and waved her fingers, flashing her gold wedding ring while she continued onward and exited the living room. "I'm a married woman. Roma, come help me get the knives, would you?"

In that moment, as Roma pushed off the wall and followed her obediently, he fell in love all over again.

5

Mrs. Gu, who owned the tailoring business that hosted the communal phone line in Zhouzhuang, came to bring Juliette an already peeled zòngzi, its sticky rice glistening in the orange sunset. Juliette mouthed her thank-you and mimed blowing Mrs. Gu a dozen kisses, making the woman chuckle as she returned to the shop counter.

Juliette took a big bite of the zòngzi. The telephone continued ringing in her ear for another half minute before a gruff voice finally picked up.

"Who is it?"

"Ah Tou, is that any way to greet me?"

On the other end of the line, Ah Tou changed his tone immediately. "Mai tàitài. What can I do for you?"

It was late evening, the sky falling darker across the township. When Juliette adjusted her shoulder so she could clamp the receiver tighter against her ear, a herd of children ran past in their haste to return for dinnertime, almost jostling her into dropping the phone. Thankfully, she had good balance.

"Relax, you're not being summoned." Ah Tou was one of their best men, happy to work at their beck and call. He was fully trusted and well connected, albeit with a very shady past that definitely had included some involvement in Suzhou's gangs. Which was great for Juliette, really, because if there was any group she knew how to talk to, it was gangsters. "I had a quick matter of interest that I figured you might know something about."

"Ask away, dàsǎo."

Juliette peered into the shop. Mrs. Gu was distracted while measuring a length of fabric.

"I killed a man earlier with an angel tattoo at the side of his neck. Chinese. Any idea if he belongs to a group of some sort?"

Ah Tou took a moment to think. "He was Chinese and he had a tattoo of an angel? Not a jīnglíng?"

"Definitely a Western angel. With the wings and the halo and the cherubic chubby cheeks—the whole shebang."

"Strange." Ah Tou made a noise, followed by the crunch of something being eaten. Juliette had probably interrupted his dinner, if his initial gruffness was any indication. "I can ask around. You need this soon?"

"As soon as possible. The last thing I need is for it to turn out to be a gang symbol and have ten of his angel-tattoo buddies coming after me for revenge."

Ah Tou huffed. "I will protect you from revenge plots, Mai tàitài."

Juliette smiled into her zòngzi. Who said criminals didn't have large hearts?

"Thank you, Ah Tou. It's appreciated. Talk soon."

She hung up, then waved goodbye to Mrs. Gu before taking her leave. As she walked her usual route home, passing the storefronts of small restaurants and sidestepping the crates left out on the canal sides, she was lost inside her own head, nibbling on the last pieces of rice stuck to the dried bamboo leaves.

Juliette almost didn't see the knife flying in her direction until the very last second.

She stepped back quickly, letting the blade clatter to a stop at her feet. It had been going at a rather low and shaky trajectory, so perhaps it would have only given her a small scratch, but she still put her hands on her hips. Her glare was not directed at Yulun, who'd thrown the wayward knife, nor at Mila, who looked mortified, but at Roma, who was overseeing the two kids.

Roma looked like he was trying not to laugh.

"Are you trying to kill me?" Juliette demanded. "*Again?*"

"At least this time I'm sending wily assassins after you," Roma replied. "Yulun, that was a good try."

"So sorry!" Yulun said to Juliette, hurrying to pick up the knife. "I was most definitely not aiming in your direction."

The target board had been pinned to the weeping willow tree, which was in the *other* direction, so Juliette could only imagine that the knife had flown out of his hand while he geared up for the throw.

"Here's a tip." Juliette scrunched up the bamboo leaves of her finished zòngzi in one hand, then used the other to push Yulun's arm straight up. "You start *here*. This arm does not need to go all the way backward for momentum. You're going to dislocate your elbow doing that."

Still, when Yulun tried again from the right position, the knife didn't land anywhere near the target.

Juliette grimaced. Roma encouraged the boy to try again. When she went to stand by Roma's side, she looked closer at the target board and saw that a few knives had landed successfully on the outer circles after all.

"Phone call has been made," she said.

"Ah Tou didn't know anything?"

"No, but he is asking." Juliette tipped her chin at the target board. "Your work?"

He puffed up like a proud mother hen. "Mila's, actually. She's a natural."

"Hardly," Mila countered, already listening from where she

stood. Her expression was intensely devoted as she geared up to throw again, putting her full attention on each attempt. "Two of them were lucky."

"You're still much better than Roma when he started out," Juliette decided.

Roma swiveled at once. "Untrue!"

"He could barely throw a marble when he was fifteen. It was horrific to witness."

"These are utter falsities. The number of times I defeated you in our marble games—"

"All right!" Juliette cut in, turning on her heel. "Let's go inside before it gets dark. I'll save you from Roma's throwing lessons with my stabbing lessons."

The clock turned one minute past midnight. Juliette had forced Mila and Yulun to take the bedroom for rest, coming close to making threats if they kept refusing out of politeness. Once they finally agreed, they had insisted on letting the door remain open, as if they were afraid of being seen as delinquents.

The two had both fallen asleep within seconds of lying down, desperately needing the rest. Maybe it would take more than one day to master the complete art of knife-stabbing, but Juliette was glad that the evening seemed to have taken their minds off the attackers on their tail. The bruise on Yulun's temple had started turning purple, which must have hurt, but he hadn't complained once.

She watched them from the doorway. An odd feeling stirred at her chest—some mixture of nostalgia and recognition. Yulun with Mila was different from Yulun who had come into the house alone. Strong-willed instead of hesitant. Bold instead of unsure. He was only seventeen. As was Mila. When she looked at the two of them sleeping, Juliette felt like she was seeing herself and Roma as their past selves, young and frantic, trying so hard to hold the world at bay and exhausting themselves in the process. Fending off attack after attack, desperately wanting to keep what they had found.

Juliette closed the door quietly.

She supposed it wasn't a direct mirror, though. She and Roma could have torn a city apart if they chose to, used their hands to crack at the cement and then dig gold from the ground, and they had turned away from it. These two didn't have that same power— these two had to ask for help, and now she and Roma had become the ones to offer it.

It was a welcome change.

Roma was at the kitchen table when Juliette wandered back out. Multiple stacks of newspapers sat piled in front of him, his eyes moving fast as he skimmed through the headlines.

"What are you looking at?" she asked.

Roma beckoned her closer without pulling his attention away from the papers. She circled around the table, then wrapped her arms around him and pressed her chin to the crook of his neck. It was a familiar position: she would often settle behind him like this while Roma wrote his letters or sorted through invoices out of nosiness at what he was doing.

"Shanghai's papers," Juliette noted, catching sight of the headlines. "Are you trying to send us back, my love?"

"Just you," Roma replied, deadpan. "Your punishment for the terrible defamation earlier."

Juliette breathed a laugh. "Sorry." She nudged her nose against his ear. "I'll make it up to you. Don't send me away."

She felt the shiver that ran along him. His gaze darted to the hallway.

"I suppose I will forgive you and hold that offer on reserve."

"Superb." Juliette bounced over to another seat at the table, taking a stack of the papers. "Now, what are we really doing?"

"Trying to find the articles that Mila mentioned," Roma answered, his focus switching back in a blink too. "But Shanghai has far too many papers."

With a toss of her hair, Juliette flicked through the first few in her pile. "We could sift out the publications that started more recently," she suggested. "Those are more propaganda than they are news."

Roma grumbled under his breath. "Still leaves a rather tall stack."

Together they scanned for a few minutes, pushing the recent publications into a pile at the end of the table. When Juliette's attention wandered briefly, her gaze went to their hallway, to that image of Yulun and Mila sleeping again.

"Roma," she said, cutting into the quiet that had settled in the kitchen. "What do you think those experiments did to the girls?"

"What do you mean?" Roma replied, still flipping through the headlines. "Other than what Mila mentioned?"

Juliette hummed a noise. "It only seems strange to me that Lourens would be experimenting with this."

She remembered what Celia had told her in a hush, almost a year after she and Roma had fled. Rosalind getting sick, then recovering with the most bizarre side effects. Now she had been recruited by the Nationalists to make use of what no one could understand—her inability to age, her rapid healing, never needing sleep—and Lourens was the one who had done it. These days, Juliette was as close as ever with Celia, but she hadn't spoken to Rosalind in years. Not since Rosalind had betrayed her and Juliette had responded in kind by keeping her tied up at a safe house and forcing her to divulge everything she knew about her then-lover. Though Juliette eventually released her cousin, she thought about their last encounter constantly. Whether there had been anything she could have done so that they hadn't left each other on such a sour note. Whether Rosalind was beating herself up over it as well, because as far as Rosalind was aware, that was the last time she'd seen Juliette *alive*.

Rosalind had been one of her best friends. As angry as Juliette was at the time, the years had mellowed her out, had meant she missed Rosalind more than she blamed her for making a mistake. Still, a long time had passed. She had no way of knowing who her cousin had become, working as a national assassin. What her cousin had been made into by Lourens's hand.

"He is an incredibly talented man," Juliette went on. He had already saved Rosalind before he met Mila, if she was understanding their time line correctly. "What is the need for these small experiments? It is a feat to have others do your bidding, very well, but from what we have heard, Lourens had invented *immortality* already. I am having trouble believing there isn't more to it, perhaps existing outside of Mila's understanding."

Roma had grown still. It took Juliette a few seconds to realize it wasn't in reaction to what she had just said, but rather that he had spotted something in the newspaper before him.

"You are correct. This is beyond belief." With a smooth swivel, Roma turned the newspaper spread so that it was facing her, allowing Juliette to scan the text. He pointed to a paragraph at the very bottom corner and read aloud:

"'. . . Initially suspected as foul play, the deaths of two Russian showgirls in the French Concession have now both been ruled as suicides. After analysis, investigators have deemed their wounds to be self-inflicted, and are working with the possibility that these cases are inspired by the madness that swept the city five years ago.'"

"What?" Juliette blurted. When Roma lifted his gaze to meet her eyes, they looked at each other with equal befuddlement. "The madness? *Our* madness? There's no chance the two girls decided to go imitating an event they weren't even in the city for. Surely it was made to look that way."

Roma folded up the paper, sliding it to the other side of the table so it wasn't in his line of sight anymore. "I can't imagine why someone's killing them by clawing their throats out either. You don't go eliminating experiment subjects if you want the research. Nor do you wait three years if it's a pressing matter of shutting them up."

The clock in the kitchen ticked loudly. It echoed across the dark green wall tiles, each passing second louder than the previous as the sound built and built. With a sigh, Juliette stretched her hand out on the table, and Roma leaned forward to lace his fingers through hers.

"I don't suppose Paul Dexter has risen from the dead to invoke chaos?" she murmured. "The other option would be Dimitri, and I would rather deal with undead Paul."

Roma's grip tightened on her hand for a moment. Then he loosened his hold, tapping his index finger against the soft pad of her palm.

"Hang on," he said. "There's an interesting thought, actually. How did we solve this the first time around?"

Juliette shuddered at the thought. "With a lot of fumbling and false assumptions."

Roma blew a puff of air at her, dismissing the answer without words. Juliette's nose scrunched immediately, pretending to look angry.

"No," Roma said before she could gather a big breath in her lungs and return the favor. "By going to the source. Imagine if we had realized earlier that Paul Dexter had the most to gain out of anyone."

Juliette understood what he was getting at. "You want to find this Mr. Pyotr fellow, don't you?"

"Shouldn't be hard for us. We have contacts in every township from here to Suzhou. My only question is how we ought to begin. He must be located in the vicinity if he is sending Mila letters without postage."

It was a quarter after midnight. Juliette tapped her chin. "We could probably break into the operating center first and see whether anyone in the area has made international calls to Vladivostok. I imagine there cannot be many, and it could reveal Mr. Pyotr's identity. Gives us more footing before we go asking about him."

Roma was already up, grabbing his jacket from the hook. "Brilliant. You're brilliant. Come on."

Juliette couldn't resist the twitch of her lips as she stood slowly, watching Roma grab her jacket too after he had put his own on. Automatically, he held hers out for her so she could slip her arms in more easily, shaking the fabric around when Juliette stayed by the table with a smile.

"Come *on*, dorogaya," he prompted.

Juliette hurried over, raising her arms and putting the jacket on. "Let's go."

6

The night stretched ominously around them, the late hour falling heavy and thick. Juliette peered over the fence, her shoes squelching in the wet grass.

"All clear?" Roma whispered.

To tell the truth, Juliette couldn't see much in the dark. There were no streetlights nearby, and the half-moon only vaguely illuminated the small telecommunications center that loomed ahead. Given that there didn't seem to be any movement in the vicinity and the building sat entirely still, she assumed that the coast was, in fact, clear.

She huffed into her hands, her breath misting visibly in a thick shroud. "It looks empty. Give me your neck."

"I beg your pardon?"

Juliette was already reaching her freezing cold hands into his collar, tucking her fingers against his bare skin. She hadn't expected the temperature to plummet this low tonight when she'd left the house without gloves. The operating center for their general area was located in a town situated a half hour's drive away from Zhouzhuang, in the nearest hub that resembled a city more than the rural countryside. Despite its comparison with their cozy township, the roads were still nowhere near Shanghai's hustle and bustle, as exemplified by the fact that there wasn't a single soul around when Roma parked under a streetlight and the two of them snuck along the shadows to get to the operating center on the next street over.

They would surely be back before morning, with plenty of time to do some investigating while Yulun and Mila rested. Juliette didn't fear for the two's safety in their house: even if Mila wasn't sleeping with Juliette's sharpest knife under the pillow, Roma had pulled out a trip wire over the front and back entranceways, activating the emergency alarm system that he had installed a year ago when an unhappy client had tried targeting their supply. Movement along any of the wires would trigger the flares installed on the rooftop. If that didn't scare the living daylights out of an intruder, nothing would.

"Is my neck warm enough for your liking?" Roma asked dryly. He barely flinched at the contact of Juliette's ice-cold hands. It wasn't as bad as her surprise attacks in the winter, when she would wrap her arms around his middle in the pretense of an embrace, only to plunge her cold hands up his shirt the moment he let his guard down.

"It is quite warm, yes."

Roma reached up to remove her hands, tucking them together to preserve the warmth she had stolen. "You can have my neck later when we're not committing crime."

"Promise?"

"Have I ever broken a promise?" Before Juliette could say a thing, Roma spun her around, walking them forward. "No—don't answer that. Rhetorical question."

"I was about to start listing every occurrence."

"That was the old me. I'm a changed man. No more broken promises or lies."

Juliette snorted. "Did you not lie to me last week about how much that giant bouquet of flowers cost?"

"*That* was for your own good, because you loved them."

"They were *ten* yuan—" Juliette shut up suddenly, hearing a faint echo to her right. She grabbed Roma, shoving them behind a tree. "Shhh!"

A sudden gust of wind blew hard, the sound drowning out any ruckus they were making. The two of them rounded the tree, then pressed tightly against the trunk to put their bodies out of view. As the leaves overhead shook, Juliette leaned out, tracking the car that was driving by. Its headlights flared along the operating center. The wheels crunched against the road's rough gravel before fading into the distance.

"What were you shushing me for?" Roma whispered after a few seconds. "You were the one talking."

"I like telling you to shut up," Juliette replied.

"Do you?"

"Absolutely." Entirely straight-faced, she added, "It gets me all hot and bothered."

Roma cleared his throat, trying very hard to look unamused by her teasing. No matter how inscrutable he kept his expression, Juliette always knew exactly when he was flustered, because he would clear his throat on a lower pitch, as if there were an itch at the base of his tongue.

"I saw a window that already looked broken." Juliette hurried out from behind the tree, circling around the fence and immediately pressing close to the building. Their surroundings were vacant enough that it was unlikely anyone would spot them, but there was no harm in being cautious. "We can break off the panel and climb through."

Roma was quick to follow in her footsteps. They found the broken window. "That may leave glass shards."

"Not to fret." Juliette reached forward to prod at the pane, trying to find the broken lines upon the glass. This had only caught her attention because someone had attempted to tape over the damage, making a large X with white paper tape that she easily peeled away. "It looks like a storage room inside. I will push the lower pane in. We can climb through easily. Then you can pin me down and—"

"*Juliette*," Roma interrupted, scandalized.

"—I can check whether there is light under the door," Juliette finished. She paused for effect. "What did you think I was going to say?"

"You—" Roma spluttered. "One does not need to be *pinned down* to check for light."

"I disagree. It helps my focus when there's physical pressure upon me. Don't you want to ensure that the rest of the building is empty?"

Roma threw his arms up into the air. Arguing with Juliette when she was already being facetious was a lost cause.

"Get working on the window. You are going to be the death of me."

Juliette grinned, taking out her switchblade. "I hope not. Benedikt will yell at me again. Cover your eyes."

She turned the weapon around and thwacked the blunt end onto the corner of the glass. Half the pane popped loose at once, falling into the room. Carefully, she wrapped her bare fingers around the rest, pulling hard until there was a perfect rectangle hollowed out from the window.

"Give me a hand, my love."

Roma was already taking his jacket off, laying it on the ledge to protect against the sharp bits and pieces that remained. Quick as she could, Juliette propped her knee onto the ledge and used his helpful push on her hips to climb through the window, landing in the storage room with a solid "*oof!*"

"Everything okay?" he asked.

"I'm getting too old for this. I think my knees creaked."

Roma climbed through too, then plucked his jacket off the

ledge. He strode toward the door, carefully opening it into the dark hallway and peering out. "My knees have been creaking since I was fifteen."

"It's all that lying you did. Aged you prematurely."

"All right, Saint Juliette. Enough about my past crimes before I start airing yours, too."

Juliette stifled a laugh. They aired each other's past crimes like it was the weekly radio programming. There was something freeing about finding humor in the matter, as if it proved that they had truly escaped what once held them captive from each other.

She grabbed Roma's arm to peer through the door as well. The hallway looked empty.

"To the left."

They slinked through the building, ears perked for movement. As expected, it was entirely empty, the clock on the wall moving its longer hand with a drowsy slowness. The main area of the operating center unfolded under the stream of moonlight, illuminating five rows of desks and headsets slung over the communication machines. Each machine had myriad wires extending from its plugs, some dangling loose and others installed tightly.

"Does no one make phone calls past midnight?" Roma wondered.

"It gets rerouted to a larger center," Juliette answered, heading for the shelf she had spotted in the corner. "Remember how early the one in Shanghai's Chinese jurisdiction would close?"

Roma looked confused, which meant he did not remember. "I think that was on your territory."

"You didn't watch what was going on in enemy territory?" She dropped to a crouch, scanning the thick logbooks stacked up on the shelf. "I watched yours."

"I watched *you*. I didn't care about what nonsense your territory was getting up to."

Roma dropped down next to her, pulling out the nearest stack.

Before Juliette could ask what their game plan was going to be, he simply set the stack on her lap, then pulled another onto his.

"This could take forever," Juliette said, craning her head to take in the whole shelf.

"Wouldn't they only keep a month's worth of logs out here, given that the previous months have already been invoiced?" He flicked her shoulder. "Start scanning. It's only September."

Juliette took a deep, dramatic breath and flipped open the first logbook. As she moved up and down the columns by moonlight, there came a point when she was scarcely reading anymore; she was *looking* in the plainest sense. Most locations in China were going to be a few characters—two or three, maybe four at most. "Fuzhou," "Shanghai," "Tianjin." On the other hand, "Vladivostok" was a whopping seven characters, so she would pause at any column entry that was overly cramped.

The logbooks started to stack up on the floor. Three piles. Five. Ten.

"Ahh!"

Roma jolted, taken aback by her sudden cry. "What is it?"

Juliette hurried to turn the logbook around, stabbing her finger at one line toward the very bottom.

"A five-minute call to Vladivostok from Happy Inn. That is only twenty minutes away from here."

It was a rural inn that Juliette knew by name because her cousin had mentioned it to her in the past. Celia hid out there sometimes between assignments if it was too much of a bother to go back to Shanghai in the short term. If they hosted Communists on occasion, then surely the word on the street cast the inn as a place to go for people who didn't want to be found.

"That's promising," Roma said. "Let's see if there are any more."

They combined efforts, with Juliette passing Roma each book and Roma doing the briefest flip through the pages. By the time they had finished the whole September stack and started to shove the logs back onto the shelf, it had only been that one entry that proved useful.

"What's the hour?" Juliette asked.

"Almost two o'clock," Roma replied.

"So we have time for another stop?"

Roma was already moving. "We do as long as you keep up."

"What!" Juliette screeched. Her heels clacked as she ran after him. "I am not any slower than you!"

7

appy Inn's front desk had been left unstaffed, but there was clearly someone on duty. Roma could hear the shuffle of footsteps in the room right behind the desk, and there was a cold cup of tea waiting too close to the edge.

"Let me jump behind the desk," Juliette whispered. She rose onto the tips of her toes to see what was hiding behind there. "I will be quick."

"No," Roma said firmly. "They could come back at any second."

"Are we merely to wait, then?"

Roma looked around the reception area of the inn, taking in the fraying wallpaper and the one hallway that led toward the rooms at the back. Understandably, there was no one else around, only the heavy hush of night and the grandfather clock in the corner, its pendulum swinging from left to right with each passing second. The red carpet under their feet might have been plush when it was first installed, but now it was so dirtied that the threads were flat and gray, murky like paint water. Mold grew in the corners of the four walls, dark clumps that decorated the wooden panels. An attempt had been made, it seemed, at etching an Art Deco border design directly onto the wood, which perhaps would have looked nicer if the squares were the same size.

"We can ask nicely for this information, so it should be no problem to wait." Delicately, as if he were removing a feral cat with her

hackles raised, he plucked Juliette's hands off the desk, walking her back a step before she lunged anyway. Then, because he wasn't sure if that would quite suffice, he took a handful of her loose hair, smoothing it over her shoulder and separating it into three sections.

"Are you . . . braiding my hair?"

"Yes," Roma answered plainly. "I'm forcing you to hold still. It also keeps getting in your eyes."

The problem with getting his wife to listen to him was that she had a penchant for *not* listening to him if the situation amused her. Big matters and serious decisions between them were effortlessly uncomplicated; they practically spoke as if they were the same person when they were trying to problem-solve together. Smaller concerns, on the other hand, were a battle between how well Roma could sweet-talk her and how stubborn Juliette decided to be in opposition. More often than not, she won.

"I didn't know you could braid hair," she remarked.

Roma made a haughty sound. "Who do you think did Alisa's hair every morning?"

"I don't think I ever saw Alisa with a braid."

"Yes, well—" The moment that Juliette tried to dart toward the desk, he abandoned the braid and his farce, weaving his fingers through her hair instead and forcibly pulling her back. "I never said I was very good. Quit that."

"I only want to have a *peek*."

"Juliette, I swear, if you don't stay still—"

She tried again. Roma yanked her hair once more, harder. Though he couldn't get a good look at her face, he could tell that Juliette was silently laughing.

It was at that moment the door behind the desk opened and the receptionist stepped out, a man who looked slightly younger, dressed in plain traditional garments and holding another cup of tea. He paused, trying to make sense of the scene before him.

Roma released his grip on Juliette's hair, shooting her a look that said, *Aren't you glad I kept you back?*

In response, Juliette turned and gave him a sly wink that wasn't fit for interpretation around company.

"Good morning," she said, sidling closer to the reception desk, now given free rein to loom over and peer at the papers. "Could you help us out? We are looking for a guest."

"It is most definitely not morning," the man replied. He set his cup down next to the one already waiting. "Who are you looking for?"

Roma approached Juliette's side. He remained wary, eyes narrowed upon the receptionist.

"He only gave me his name as Mr. Pyotr," she answered. "I don't suppose anyone here matches?"

"Mhmmm . . . no, no one does."

Juliette cast Roma a glance. Roma lifted his brow, returning her suspicion.

"You didn't check your books."

"No need, I already know." The receptionist took a sip of tea, then looked up at them as if to ask why they were still standing there. "The name holds no familiarity."

Juliette leaned over the desk. "Give me the guest book then. I will check myself."

"Absolutely not," the young man replied. The first signs of ill-tempered fire entered his eye. Juliette had mentioned on the car ride over that this place was also a political hideout, which meant the people behind the desk would be well suited to that work. Somehow, Roma doubted that the information would be handed over easily.

"I'm going to grab it," Juliette said to Roma, making no effort to whisper or even lower her voice.

"Excuse me?" The receptionist started to reach under his desk.

"Xiǎo huǒzi," Roma warned him, his eyes tracking the motion.

He knew exactly what Juliette was planning and what she wanted him to do in the seconds following, but if the receptionist wanted to avoid a traumatizing experience, he could simply put his hands in the air. "You really don't want to do that."

He did it anyway: the receptionist pulled a gun out. Pointed it.

And quicker than the eye could follow, Juliette had him disarmed, whacking down hard on the barrel and spinning the weapon around so that it was in her palm instead, pointed at the man.

In the aftermath, while the man spluttered in shock, hands held up to prevent being shot, Roma reached forward, plucking the guest book up and bringing it near.

"The telephone call was made two weeks ago," Juliette said.

"Yes, I remember," Roma replied lightly, acting as if they were merely discussing the rice needing to be lifted off the stove. He flipped the pages, looking over the names. It was very likely that Mr. Pyotr would be using an alias, but he had faith that there would be *some* kind of giveaway.

"Find anything?"

Roma blinked at the page. "Actually . . . yes." He turned the guest book around, pointing to the column for two weeks ago. There was no Pyotr, but . . .

"Why are there so many Russian names here? Did you get a whole group in?"

"For heaven's sake, what's it to you?" the man answered. He heaved a defeated sigh. "Yes, there was a whole group. They left earlier today."

With her weapon still pointed, Juliette scrunched her brow. They could try to weigh whether the man was telling the truth, but the information was fairly benign. He wasn't really giving up much by revealing it.

"You really could have opened with that." She looked over at Roma again while he set down the guest book. The two of them had

a silent exchange, questions passing in the most minute changes of their expressions.

Was it that Mr. Pyotr had brought a whole squadron of people and logged himself here with an alias? Or had Mr. Pyotr hired them, and he himself was located in Vladivostok, hence the phone call there? There were too many possibilities and not enough information. The people in this guest book could be a dead end at worst and multiple vague leads at best.

Roma reached out to tap Juliette's elbow.

"Keep him here," he said lowly. "I'm going to look around."

"No!" the receptionist protested immediately. "You cannot *look around*. Our guests need privacy—"

"Don't even think about it." Juliette waved the gun, gesturing for him to lean back from the step he had been about to take around the desk. "Stay still."

"I am not scared of—"

Juliette fired at his feet, craning her arm over the desk to aim. The man yelped. One bullet embedded a hairsbreadth beside his shoe, charring a hole into the carpet.

"That was the first warning." She huffed. "Do we want to test how many warnings I have in me?"

"This is *absurd*—"

Roma hurried off, knowing Juliette had the mild threats handled. As he walked farther into the inn, he glided his fingers along the wall, picking up dust from the wallpaper. It was only a thin smattering, but it meant the inn received infrequent cleanings, which probably didn't matter much to the patrons here if they didn't have a host of other options nearby. On his way up the road, Roma thought the building hadn't looked very large either, situated beside a small creek that ran along its right side.

He tried some of the doors into the rooms. Found most to either be locked from the inside, with snores echoing along the

loose flooring, or opening only to a tiny empty space with a broom inside. Back at the reception area, he could hear Juliette talking loudly, adopting that theatric tone she used when she was yammering merely to wind someone up.

One of the doors finally opened under his palm. He stepped in, examining the moonlit interior. The bedsheets were stripped, but they had been left in a pile on the floor, as if a maid had come by to do the brunt of the work but a launderer had yet to finish the second half of the job. Other than that, the room was vacant. When Roma ran his finger along the bare wooden table, there was no dust at all.

Someone had recently finished their stay here. It had been cleaned no less than a few hours ago.

"Hmmm . . ."

He backed out of the room and tried the one next to it. Juliette's voice wafted over again, having moved on to the topic of . . . *childbirth*? What on earth was she talking to the receptionist about?

With a quick shake of his head to focus on his task, Roma rifled through another pile of stripped bedsheets, peering around the room to find an almost identical setup. Perhaps the bedsheets being left behind meant that though the room had been sorted and inventoried, the used items had yet to be discarded. So maybe . . .

He spotted a small trash can in the corner. Peered in. Nothing except a single cigarette. But now he was intrigued. These rooms still held the remnants of the guests who had last resided here.

Roma continued checking through all the rooms that easily opened under his palm, groping his hands around the empty wardrobes and patting the corners of the windowpanes. In one of the final rooms down the hall, at the very end of the inn, he entered and immediately smelled cigarette smoke, potent enough that he wasn't surprised when he peered into the trash can and found six end stubs. Beneath it, he spotted several ripped pieces of paper, some of the corners singed and charred.

His nose wrinkled. Grimacing, Roma reached in and fished the pieces out. No matter how disgusting it was to be going through someone else's trash, he reminded himself of Yulun's panicked face and Mila's sad frown, then started to join up the six jagged fragments.

```
No. 143
Invoice for Services
Description: A hundred yuan
Pay to: ███████████
```

The writing was incredibly faint. Though much of it had been obscured by the cigarette burns, Roma rubbed his finger against some of the legible parts and confirmed that its coloring wasn't because the pen had run out of ink—no, this was a piece of copy paper that had been pressed underneath the original to duplicate exactly what had been written on top. It must have been thrown out after they received their money and didn't need the copy for their records anymore.

Roma scooped up the invoice pieces and put them back in the trash can. There were no identifying details to be found, but it *was* written in Russian, which confirmed it was related to the call to Vladivostok. A hundred yuan was a considerable sum of money. If the occupant of this room had been issuing invoices to be paid in such amounts, surely it had to be for something significant.

With his head pulsating with questions, Roma exited the room, his perusal of Happy Inn complete.

". . . not at all— Oh, hello, my love," Juliette greeted, breaking off mid-ramble. "Did you have a good search?"

Roma approached the desk casually, hands in his pockets, while

Juliette still had the gun out. He waited for a few seconds before saying, "It was adequate. Good conversation?"

"Absolutely," she replied, at the same time that the receptionist grumbled, "*No.*"

Juliette flashed a grin. In that expression, she silently asked Roma if they were ready to depart, and Roma gave the barest nod that only she could catch. He leaned forward to look at the guest book again and, thinking it might come into use, tore out the relevant page.

"We will keep this, thank you."

Before the receptionist could splutter in protest, Juliette was reaching into her coat pocket and pulling out a wad of cash. She took a step back, then set the money on the floor with the gun on top. "We will get out of your way now," she added, sounding as pleasant as ever. "Have a good morning."

"It is not morning!" the man called after them, aggrieved.

Roma and Juliette were already outside, ducking away from view before the receptionist could follow them out. With a careful eye for rocks in his path, Roma hurried down the steep grassy decline, finding his footing a second before Juliette and lunging to catch her elbow before she could teeter on her own landing.

"Thank you," she breathed. "I don't suppose you stumbled onto Mr. Pyotr's birth certificate alongside a manifesto for his experiments?"

"Unfortunately not." Roma tucked her hair behind her ear. "I found a copy of an invoice. The group who stayed here must have made the call to Vladivostok, and someone among them was also asking for a payment of a hundred yuan."

Juliette's brow furrowed. "I don't know what that means."

Roma sighed. "Neither do I, to be frank. I think we may have exhausted this route. Let's go wide again tomorrow." He paused. "After the shipments come, that is. We have incoming deliveries."

They had new problems on their hands, but their business did not stop. They still had to make their living somehow.

A thick cloud swallowed up the moonlight, drowning them in darkness for a few seconds. He could feel Juliette's shoulders sag, using sheer intuition before wisps of silver light streamed through the clouds again and he confirmed that her posture had indeed slumped.

"I guess we knew this was a long shot." She kicked a rock. "Home?"

"Home," Roma agreed. "Are we sharing the sofa?"

Juliette reached for him, curling a hand around his upper arm and latching tight as they started to walk.

"We can even cuddle if you ask nicely," she said.

8

She was dreaming that god-awful dream again, and it always started the same way.

First, the smell of smoke and dust, heavy in the air and at the back of her throat. If dreams weren't supposed to make sense, Juliette wished that hers would scramble this opening a little instead of re-creating her memories down to every last visceral sense: the sights and the sounds and the horrific screaming that had ricocheted through the blood-filled streets.

There she was, standing on the streets of Zhabei—in the north of Shanghai's city center, surrounded by carnage. Her feet rooted to the concrete, legs impossibly heavy. An all-consuming feeling of *"Go! Go! Go!"* screamed louder inside her each time this dream sequence started, slapped four years into the past for the end to play out differently, taking every fear she had imagined and amplifying them tenfold.

The monsters were ambling closer. In her hand, her lighter felt like it would burn through her skin, searing right to bone.

"We must move fast," she heard herself say, warped and distant, as if it were coming from the skies instead of her own throat. *"Do you understand me?"*

Roma always materialized next to her at that moment, but standing farther than he had been in reality. Her panic surged; she was terrified that he wouldn't catch her signal when she pointed toward the drain covering three paces away, that Dimitri might spot her gesture instead, catch on to her plan, and take the same way out. They couldn't leave unless he was gone. Every bit of havoc he had wrought in the city needed to be burned to the ground.

I love you. I love you. I love you.

Sometimes, in the dream, she remembered that Roma had been holding her hand, squeezing her fingers to communicate his encouragement. Sometimes she didn't, and it wasn't until the moment she threw the lighter that her memories reminded her it was Roma who had tugged her forward first, already moving while Juliette instinctively waited to watch her lighter make contact with the vaccine bags. There was no time. If Roma had been a second slower in tugging the drain covering aside; if Juliette had hesitated before shoving Roma through, yelling *"Go!"*; if Roma hadn't stubbornly reached for her elbow while falling so that she was dragged through with him, the two of them landing hard in the sewer grates just as the explosion tore free . . . then they wouldn't have made it out.

In this dream, Juliette hadn't thought to push Roma through first. And in that second of delay, as he turned back to look at her . . .

Juliette jerked awake, a trail of tears already streaming down her cheeks. For a moment, the unfamiliar environment sent a wave of alarm into her body, half-conscious deliriousness slowing her comprehension. Then she felt an arm tighten around her waist and a pressure on her shoulder. Roma, nudging closer from behind, setting his chin upon her.

"Darling Juliette," he said drowsily. "Are you crying?"

Her alarm started to ease, awareness flooding back. They were sleeping in the living room, tucked among the cushions on the sofa. Yulun and Mila were in the bedroom because they were being pursued by dangerous people, and in this scramble to keep them safe, Juliette was thinking about the past again, and thinking about the past always brought the dreams.

"I'm not crying," Juliette sniffed, turning on the cushions so that she could face him.

Roma hadn't opened his eyes. Somehow he still managed to raise his hand and brush away the dampness on her cheeks with perfect accuracy.

"You're allowed to cry," he said, his eyes still closed, voice husky and scratchy. "I cry all the time."

"That you do."

They hadn't drawn the blinds when they went to sleep, too tired to do anything except collapse. Cloud-covered moonlight streamed through the windows, illuminating shapes and outlines in the living room. Juliette, with a soft exhale, slid a little lower along the sofa so that she could tuck herself against Roma's chest.

With that terrible scene still fresh in her mind's eye, she knew there was a chance it would drag her back the moment she dropped her guard. But the hour was clearly too early—or late, depending on the standard they were judging by—to rise for the day and shake off her dreams, so she squeezed her eyes shut again, holding Roma tighter and focusing on the steady thrum of his heartbeat under her ear. He smoothed his hand from her waist to her arm in response, tracing lazy lines upon her skin. As simple as the gesture was, her breathing slowed instinctively, following the up-down pace of the motions.

"I had the dream again," Juliette whispered into his shirt.

"The explosion?"

"Yes."

"What happened this time?"

"I lost you." She breathed in, and a hitch stole her breath, snagged in her throat, turned everything sour. "In all the worst ones, I always lose you."

When they'd hit the sewer, it had sounded like the world was caving in. The metal walls shook until Juliette feared the very structure would collapse on them, dirt and dust raining down while the heat of the blast blew through the open drain covering. Her mind barely felt coherent. She was half convinced that she had died and this was the underworld, the sound of trickling water and rancid smells running under the grates that were pressed into the left side of her body. She didn't know when she had hit her head, but blood was trickling down her brow and getting into her eye.

The shaking continued for a short eternity. Then: silence.

"Juliette," Roma had breathed, lifting his head cautiously. He had cuts along his cheek, and deliriously, Juliette reached out to run her finger against the deepest one, horrified at the slash of red, as if that was their most pressing problem. "Juliette, we need to go."

"What?" she said, barely registering his words. Her ears were ringing terribly. Each sound in the real world echoed twice and then got eaten by a buzzing in her head.

Roma grabbed her elbow, yanking her to her feet. The sewer pipe didn't extend high enough for them to stand properly.

"They can't find us here, dorogaya. What's going to happen when they find us here?"

And just like that, Juliette snapped back into alertness, the last few hours before the explosion flashing back into her head at rapid speed. The execution order on the Montagovs. Her rebellion against her own family. It wasn't over because Dimitri was gone. The soldiers would kill Roma on the Scarlet Gang's orders. The Scarlet Gang would drag her back and punish her.

"Let's go," Juliette commanded, pulling herself back through the drain. Her fingers burned on the charred metal, but she gritted her teeth and labored through it. Large flames remained at the scene. Burned bodies, unrecognizable past their skeletal shapes. As soon as Roma clambered out, Juliette pushed the drain back into place, and then they ran, deep into the city.

For almost a week afterward, they laid low at an abandoned safe house on Thibet Road, recovering and waiting and asking each other again and again if they were certain. At last, while their gravestones were being carved elsewhere in the city, they made up their minds, and Celia found the transport to usher them out of Shanghai in the dead of night.

Juliette craned her head, letting her eyes focus in the dim moonlight. She reached for Roma's cheek, then smoothed her thumb along a faint scar on the highest point.

Though they were here now, the day of that explosion had been the last day they spent alive as Shanghai's infamous heirs. The people who had clambered out from that drain were changed—mere shadow selves. They emerged back into the world, deciding that they had done what they could for their city and it was time to choose themselves, at long last.

They could never let go of Shanghai entirely, though. Roma was waiting to summon Alisa; Juliette thought about her parents more often than she cared to admit. She knew that she would never make contact again, that unlike Roma's relationship with her sister, her goodwill with her parents had been severed entirely when she defied them. All the same, there was an aching crevasse in her body that missed their presence, out of habit and familiarity that she would never be able to fully erase.

"You won't ever lose me," Roma murmured in the present. "You made me do a pinkie promise, remember?"

"Actually," Juliette corrected, "I was promising you, but you never promised me."

Roma's eyes finally fluttered open. In that narrow strip of silver streaming through the window, his pupils were so large that his gaze was wholly black.

"I would have assumed," he said slowly, "that our marriage vows shortly afterward implied a returned promise."

Juliette stubbornly stuck her pinkie out. With a huff of air, Roma dragged his hand over and curled their pinkies together.

"You won't ever lose me," he repeated, sounding so serious even with the jest in their actions. "And I love you, to have and to hold as my unlawfully wedded wife, until the universe itself goes *poof.*"

Juliette's lip twitched. "Stop changing your vows. Your first ones were better."

"It's late, lǎopó. I need functioning thought to be eloquent."

The remnants of her dream felt further away now. Distant, like the city was.

"Go back to sleep," Juliette said. She released their pinkies. "You can barely keep your eyes open."

"As long as you sleep too." He made a noise of protest, then retrieved her hand before it could escape and propped her palm against his chest in the limited space between their bodies. "I will be right here if you wake up again."

Juliette searched his gaze. Nodded. In response, Roma dropped a kiss on her forehead, short and sweet and tired.

Then he waited, looking at her instead of going to sleep.

"What?" Juliette asked.

"You haven't kissed me back," he said.

Juliette held in her titter. Feigning a begrudging sigh, she returned the kiss on his lips. No matter how she pretended, the seconds she lingered there told the truth.

When Juliette pulled away, Roma made a satisfied smile and settled to return to sleep.

"Such a big baby," she said fondly.

9

Despite her lack of rest, Juliette was up at the crack of dawn, chopping shrimp in the kitchen. The dreams hadn't returned when she fell asleep again, her unconsciousness offering the comforting void of nothing until the first hint of day brushed against her eyes.

Roma was still fast asleep in the living room. He had one arm dangling over the edge of the sofa and the other propped under his head as a new makeshift pillow after Juliette extricated herself. The morning had only started to emit light, and the world outside hovered in a purplish tone that let dreaming and waking prevail on the same plane.

Juliette brushed a handful of shrimp into a bowl. She was quite a good cook, contrary to natural assumption—or at least she was better at cooking than Roma was at driving. Which, given, was a low bar to reach, but she had yet to burn anything too badly.

Just as she started on the next clump of shrimp, she heard the front door open. Her knife stilled, head tilted to take in the sound. As soon as footfalls entered the living room and started to pad in her direction, however, Juliette relaxed, recognizing the steps and putting her knife down.

"Welcome!" she crowed, opening her arms when Celia entered the kitchen.

"Hello to you too," her cousin returned, meeting the embrace.

She drew away with her nose wrinkled. "Did you kick your husband onto the sofa?"

"That's ridiculous—I would never kick him onto the sofa," Juliette replied. "If he ever angers me, a better punishment would be for him to continue sleeping next to me, feeling the power of my wrath."

Celia shook her head. "You two stress me out. Why are the trip wires at the door pulled?"

"The answer is a long story that would stress you further, frankly." Juliette pulled her cousin closer to the counter. "We have young guests taking the bedroom, hence Roma on the sofa. Now come help me with the jiǎozi so we can feed them."

"Shrimp and garlic chives," Celia observed of the ingredients already laid out. She looked around. "Are you putting eggs in too? I will whisk."

Already prepared, Juliette reached into the cabinet below the sink and offered a big bowl before turning back to the shrimp. The sunrise was creeping higher, which helped her see what she was doing tremendously more than the half-painted dawn did. Though she could have turned on a light, she didn't want to disturb Roma's sleep, because chances were that he would stir at the bulbs flaring on and come help her no matter how tired he actually was.

"What brings you over today?" Juliette asked while Celia rummaged through the shelves. "Missed me?"

If her cousin was going to drop in, it was always during these early hours. It reduced the chances of her being seen, and it lessened the amount of questions she got from her operation teams. In these recent few months, Celia had been posted nearby, right in Taicang, which was north of Shanghai and a reasonable drive away. Though she came by more often because of the proximity, she always had to be careful that her mission partner didn't get suspicious. Her greater operation team swapped around, but Oliver

Hong did not, because the Communists had paired them up as a permanent two-person unit. On days when Celia tried to visit but Oliver decided to accompany her, she had to play it off as wanting to see Zhouzhuang's markets, and Juliette would hover nearby giving a cheerful nod.

"I figured it had been some time since I last saw you," Celia answered. "I also wanted to ask if you have been reading about what's happening in Shanghai."

"Recently?"

Juliette nudged the shrimp pieces to the side of the cutting board. Usually, she tended to avoid the papers reporting on Shanghai. It wasn't that she wanted to keep ignorant; it was only that it felt strange to be uninvolved in the city's affairs when overseeing them was all she had known at one point in her life. As happy as she was out here, sometimes she would stumble upon an article that mentioned her parents, and then there would be a sour taste on her tongue that she wouldn't be rid of for days afterward.

"Rosalind has been investigating a series of civilian murders," Celia said, taking Juliette's nonanswer for a *no*. "They're close to pinning down a Japanese company for being responsible, but I think there might be something shifty going on among the Nationalists, too. You may want to be careful with your trade for a while."

Juliette made a noise under her breath, signaling her understanding. Though Juliette didn't like reading the papers, she and Roma were still very well informed as to what was going on in Shanghai. They employed plants who would report information where it was relevant. In fact, according to a recent letter, they had someone inside the very company where Rosalind was currently undercover.

"We will be careful," Juliette assured. "There's enough trouble around here to keep us busy."

Celia set the chopsticks beside the bowl. "I did see more vehicles than usual on my way in."

Juliette's knife paused on the cutting board. "Oh?"

"I passed a group who didn't seem like residents either. They were holding a map between them discussing where to go. Russian-speaking. Maybe five or six."

"What!" Juliette dropped the knife entirely. "Where? By the township edge?"

Celia blinked widely, clearly confused about why Juliette cared so much. "Nearer the incoming main road, away from the canals. Do you know them? I heard one call another by the name of Ilya."

Juliette hurried into the living room, diving for the coffee table, where they had left the sheet ripped out from Happy Inn's guest book. The motion stirred Roma awake. While he propped himself up on his elbow in sleep-addled confusion, she squinted to read the messy handwriting, turning the paper for the morning light. *There*—the third one was an Ilya.

"They've found her."

"Who?" Celia demanded. "Juliette, what's going on?"

"Seconding that," Roma croaked, pushing his hair out of his face. "Hello, biǎojiě."

Celia waved amiably. Meanwhile, Juliette kicked her slippers off and stomped into a pair of shoes—flat ones, suited for running. "Please stay here. Shoot anyone who comes in through the door."

"Excuse me?" Celia spluttered. "I didn't bring a gun!"

Juliette adjusted her left shoe. "There's one under the coffee table!"

"I—" Celia ducked to look under the table, plucking the weapon out. "I need to get back, Juliette!"

"Okay, you can get back in ten minutes—pleasepleaseplease, thank you, my most beloved cousin." Juliette flung open the door, hopping over the trip wire. "Roma, meet me by the open markets. I will get a head start."

"What?" he barely managed.

Juliette was already outside, edging along the canal and making way for the stone bridge. She started in a steady run, passing the row of houses on the other side of the water. Mrs. Fan was outside tending to her potted plants, her head snapping up when Juliette approached.

"Fan nǎinai," Juliette greeted, slowing only a fraction. "Can you scream very loudly if you see a group of men approaching?"

Mrs. Fan blinked. "Oh. Oh, I suppose so."

Juliette surged ahead, ducking under a collection of laundry lines and swerving onto a lesser-used route. By nature of being a water township, most of Zhouzhuang was more long-winding than necessary, the canals uncrossable until there was a bridge that provided a path over water. But Juliette had been here for long enough to know exactly which canals kept a supply of wooden planks by their edges—tossed over for easy passage, as long as you didn't lose your balance and fall—and which canals had extra stone steps jutting into the water, narrowing the distance to the other side and allowing for jumping.

In no time she was approaching the main road, drawing farther from the waterways and hurrying along the market tents. Only two or three vendors had set up shop, the hour too early to bring proper sunlight over the horizon. She didn't rush in her search. If Celia had spotted the men here, then there were only a certain number of routes they could have taken from this point.

It was more useful to think about how she would make her approach. As she passed a stall, Juliette snatched a rag left to dry on a bamboo rung. Then she swiped a hammer, frowning when the handle chipped paint onto her palm.

The hammer would perhaps be more intimidating to swing around if she weren't dressed so nicely. Juliette dropped the tool back down, determining that the gun in her pocket would probably suffice.

Voices.

She paused. Listened. Her feet coming down silently, Juliette backtracked and followed into an alley, catching the first glimpse of movement. There were various passageways here that led into open courtyards and private gardens with expansive gazebos. Right as another bit of movement flashed ahead, she hurried into a parallel alley, pressed close to the wall and surging forward so that she was moving with the group. She proceeded carefully with a wall between them for a few minutes, before the next opportunity presented itself and a small alley connected the two.

Juliette counted to five. Then she darted into their alley and grabbed the man lingering at the back of their group, clapping her rag to his mouth and kicking the back of his knees to send him off-balance. Before the rest of his group could take notice or turn around to investigate what that faintly muffled noise had been, she dragged him in the other direction by his head, barging into someone's courtyard and using her momentum to keep going until they were past a set of wooden doors, blocking sound from the alley.

The moment she paused, the man bucked hard, pushing the rag and her grip off his face. By then, Juliette had already delivered a hearty blow to his head with her elbow, sending him to the ground just long enough for her to grab her gun. He whirled around. Blinked up. She pointed her weapon at his face.

"Hello," she said, slightly breathless from the struggle. "You have five seconds to talk."

The man stilled. She wondered which one he was. If not Ilya, then surely another of the names from the guest book.

His eyes moved to the left. Maybe-Ilya put his hands up to show goodwill.

Then his feet kicked out, striking Juliette hard in the shin. She wheeled back, but it wasn't enough to tip her over completely, and she lunged forward again with ten times more conviction, jamming the barrel of her gun right to his forehead before he could sit up properly. Her knees scraped into the dirt. There were small pebbles digging into her skin.

"Listen very carefully," Juliette hissed, switching to Russian. Her tone dropped low; her words bit out in a growl. The group would discover he was missing and circle back before long. She needed to be fast. "I have at least five bullets left in this gun and I can make this a very painful process for each of your limbs. Answer one very simple question: Who sent you to kill Milyena?"

She cringed a little sometimes when she had to bring out the former gangster heiress. But effective tactics were effective tactics.

"You—"

"*Five.*"

"What—"

"*Four.*"

"It's not—"

Juliette's finger started to press down on the trigger. "*Three.*"

"We are not the ones killing them—*what* is your *problem?*"

And in that split second of confusion, while Juliette's pressure eased a fraction, Maybe-Ilya whirled out of range and struck up hard with his fist. Both sides of her face suddenly stung like hell: the left from getting hit and the right as it collided with the rough ground.

Juliette recovered fast. The man was drawing his own weapon; she turned hers around and attempted a strike, not wanting to shoot until absolutely necessary lest it draw his group's notice. The heel of her gun took him off-balance, only the man had already fired, and the bullet whizzed narrowly past her arm, striking the courtyard wall.

"Are you not the ones hunting each of them down?" she hissed.

Maybe-Ilya tried to shoot again, rising onto his knees. Juliette finally returned fire, a bullet missing his side as he dove back to the ground in haste.

"Idiot girl, do not blame *us*. If anything, we need the girls alive. We are doing our damn best to knock them out and keep them unharmed." When the man fired again, Juliette moved a second too slow, her breath coming heavy. A red-hot bullet grazed her shoulder. She flinched, and as she drew her elbow closer to keep the wound unmoving, the man attacked, pushing her into the ground as she had done to him before, gun to her head.

"Explain yourself," she demanded, even in her precarious position.

She smacked her head up, tried to swivel. With a curse, Maybe-Ilya made a face so ferocious that spittle had gathered at the corners of his mouth.

"We are merely on a retrieval mission that you are interrupting," he spat. "It is not our fault that they are brainwashed to kill themselves the moment we get near."

Juliette froze in horror. He brought his gun down, intending to strike her hard and knock her out.

But before the arc could finish, Maybe-Ilya went limp. Someone from above hauled him right off her, carelessly tossing his slumped body aside.

"Christ, Juliette, you could have waited *two minutes*."

Her vision focused on her savior, framed by the morning sun. Roma had never looked so beautiful, even while he was glaring at her. She most definitely had blood on her lip when she grinned in return.

"Stop looking so happy that you got beaten up."

Roma reached down, hauling her onto her feet with a strong hand.

"I did not get beaten up," Juliette corrected, finding her balance. "My opponent looks just as bad as me, so it would be more accurate to say that I got into a fierce scuffle."

It didn't seem like Roma was very entertained by her levity. He fussed over the dirt smears on her elbows, trying to brush her clean.

"Don't worry about the rest of them," he assured her as he nudged her hair out of her face, wincing at the bruising that was surely appearing along her forehead. "I knocked them out without exchanging too many pleasantries. I figured you would get the information."

"That I did." Juliette blew a piece of hair out of her eyes. "How did you know I ducked in here?"

"I have an internal compass that centers on you instead of true north."

Juliette gave him a wry look.

"Well," Roma added, gently padding his fingers along the ridge of her jaw, "I also saw the signs of a struggle in the dirt outside and figured you had dragged someone in here. What did he say?"

The man she had dragged in—maybe Ilya, maybe not—lay prone with one arm at an awkward angle. He was going to have terrible pins and needles when he woke up. For a moment, as Juliette walked up to him slowly and used her foot to straighten his arm, she considered pointing her gun and killing him, securing some safety for Mila in the quickest possible way. Only then his words echoed once more in her mind.

We are merely on a retrieval mission. . . . It is not our fault that they are brainwashed to kill themselves the moment we get near.

It hadn't sounded like a lie, which meant killing him would be fruitless. The two girls in Shanghai had been marked as suicides, after all. The other two girls hadn't left signs of a struggle, only blood everywhere. At last, it seemed they had finally gotten an answer for what had been done to Mila in the facility.

"Depending on which way we look at it," Juliette answered, putting her gun away, "either something that improves this situation or makes it much, much worse."

10

They had tied them up. Roma had watched with some light concern as Juliette got overly enthusiastic with the task, going as far as to wrap rope around one of the men until he looked near mummified.

Once they were secured and still knocked out, Roma had left Juliette to watch over them while he hurried back to their house. Zhouzhuang was small enough that it took no more than twenty minutes to wake Mila up and bring her to the alley, where she approached each unconscious man cautiously and inspected their faces.

"No," Mila had answered after a moment. "I don't recognize any of these people."

"Then I have bad news about what they're doing down here," Juliette said.

It is not our fault that they are brainwashed to kill themselves the moment we get near. Roma had barely comprehended the words while Juliette was explaining. Mila was still terribly pale, digesting the news by sitting down at the end of the alley, staring at her own hands in horror. He figured that she needed a moment, so he tilted his head at Juliette, asking her to step a few paces away with him so they could talk out of her hearing range.

"Are you all right?" Juliette asked.

He cupped her chin in concern. "You're the one with the bruised face, and you are asking me?"

"I know this hurts you more than it hurts me." She scrunched her nose in jest, then immediately winced when it pulled her muscles. The fabric of her dress was entirely brown-red at her shoulder, but the color had stopped spreading, which meant she wasn't bleeding anymore.

"Don't be a comedian," Roma muttered. "I really do have phantom physical pain watching you."

"You can patch me up at home." Juliette glanced back, her attention drifting to Mila at the end of the alley. "What do you think all this means?"

"I'm thinking that if the girls have been brainwashed into killing themselves, then it was probably the two scientists at the facility who are responsible."

Their theory had started with Mr. Pyotr coming after her, but there was no chance that he didn't *know* about this mechanism. If anything, he really was warning her.

They are coming.

"So who are the people coming after them?" Juliette mused aloud. "It's almost as if we found their presence at the inn by accident."

"No, not by accident," Roma countered. "We were following anyone who made contact with Vladivostok. It's only that we assumed this Mr. Pyotr would be the one nearby with ties there."

"Because of the facility." Juliette shivered slightly, her head tilting to watch the sun rise over the building, bringing proper morning at last. She usually pinned her hair back in the daytime, but there hadn't been a chance this morning, and so the wisps blew along her shoulders, fluttering like petals with each soft wave of wind. "So it has to be the facility who are sending these men, or else there's no reason they made that call at the inn. He called it a retrieval mission. The facility wants the girls back."

Roma resisted the urge to lie down in the alley. He wanted to do exactly what Mila was doing and sink against the wall.

That hundred-yuan invoice had probably been for the facility, as requested payment for these retrieval services. But each of the other girls had been failed retrievals because they had killed themselves first, and if Shanghai's newspapers were to be believed, their method of death mimicked the madness five years ago, which had caused people to *gouge their own throats out*.

"I really don't like the puzzle pieces that are being tossed around here," he said. "The facility is after the girls and wants to snatch them back, fine. Casual everyday human trafficking. But throat-gouging as the built-in defense mechanism?"

That was very much *not* included in usual trafficking endeavors.

Juliette was quiet for a bit. "Roma," she said when she turned her gaze away from the rooftops. "Don't you find it a little peculiar that this defense mechanism is something we are so familiar with?"

"It's not really the madness," he replied, knowing in an instant what she was talking about. "No insects."

"But if this precise act has been brainwashed into the girls, it could only have been done by someone who was inspired by it," she said. "And there is one person involved who *did* witness the madness."

That one person, of course, being Lourens Van Dijk.

Roma cursed under his breath. A bird landed in the alley, feathers ruffling as it silently hopped around the tied-up men.

"Do we need to find him?" he asked. "Is that where the root of this lies? I doubt the facility will stop coming after her only because these hired men have failed."

"Lourens is impossible to find." Juliette didn't hesitate with the claim. "Rosalind has tried, believe me. Or believe Celia, I suppose."

Though he and the old scientist had never been close, Roma had still seen him often while going in and out of the labs for gangster business. It was hard to believe the same Lourens who hated birds and liked jazz music could be that callous. That he might create an instruction like this.

"We will figure it out," Roma decided. Maybe if he said it confidently enough, he could will it into existence. "In the meantime, take Mila home. I will call Ah Tou and ask him to deal with . . ." He gestured vaguely at the unconscious men in the alley.

"All right." Juliette winced. "Celia is probably fretting up a storm."

"On the contrary, she was sitting on the sofa taking up my knitting project when I went in to fetch Mila." Roma touched her face in goodbye, then turned to go, calling back: "But you should hurry, because it'll be embarrassing if she finishes that sweater for me."

"Wéi?"

Roma started, his attention having wandered off while the phone rang. "Ah Tou. It's me."

"Lǎobǎn," Ah Tou greeted in an instant. Roma could practically imagine the man straightening up on the other side, brushing his jacket clean. No matter how many times he and Juliette tried to tell Ah Tou to tone it down, that they weren't gang bosses and didn't need to be treated as such, Ah Tou insisted on addressing them in that manner. Though, to be fair, Juliette probably quite enjoyed being called dàsǎo.

"I'm going to need your help in Zhouzhuang," Roma said. "Bring some people. Does Leilei still have those god-awful brass rings?"

"She won't even take them off to shower."

"Great. Bring her especially. I need some men roughed up."

Ah Tou didn't question the instruction in the slightest. "How bad?"

"Enough so that they'll flee the area and never come back. No broken bones. I'll allow a swollen kneecap or two." Roma paused, considering. It wasn't as if that would stop whoever had sent them, because there were probably plenty of outlaws needing work these days who could pick up the mantle after this group. Especially when there was substantial money on the line. "Maybe try to get a name out of them too. Ask who sent them. But I doubt you will get much."

"Understood," Ah Tou replied. "Oh, and I asked around for Mai tàitài. An angel tattoo around these parts isn't an insignia of loyalty to a gang, it's the mark of a former mercenary group. My source is shocked they're still around. They used to take British funding before the group collapsed when the civil war started."

Roma put his hand on his forehead. He dragged it down his face. That meant the first man who had attacked Mila was an entirely different group to the Russians in the alley. For the love of God.

"Do you know how many members might still be around?"

Or rather, how many might have known about the first man's task and would come sniffing around to find out what happened to him.

"My guess is not many. Again, they have dwindled drastically in number."

"All right," Roma said. If they were lucky, maybe the mercenary group had dwindled down to their last member. "Are you on your way?"

"On it, lǎobǎn."

Roma put the phone down. He waited there for a moment, feeling the wind on his face and the morning sun rising and rising. Sometimes he frightened himself with how easy it was to make these calls and deliver these instructions. Not only because morals became a slippery slope, but because a certain authority slipped into his voice when he wasn't watching, and he never thought that would have come so naturally. He used to think he would have made a terrible leader to the White Flowers; at every misstep as the heir, his father had chided him, telling him that he couldn't seem to do a thing right. Of course Roma believed it—he wouldn't have tried so hard to prove himself otherwise.

Look at him now. Perhaps in some other reality, one where he hadn't ever met Juliette, he was miserable and unhappy heading the White Flowers but doing a fantastic job.

"Mai xiānshēng, catch!"

A ball came hurtling toward his face. With barely any time to react, Roma threw his hands up and knocked the ball out of the way, gaping bewildered at the young boy who had thrown it.

"What have we said," he chided, "about throwing objects at me?"

"That I should keep doing it!"

The boy ran off cackling. Roma picked up the ball, wiping any appearance of his true amusement from his expression, because while every child in this township adored bullying him, he could hardly give them permission to keep doing it.

"Aiya, watch where you're going!"

Another voice carried across the canal as the boy turned a sharp corner, almost running into the man there. Roma followed after the boy, nodding his apology to the postman delivering letters, then rolled his eyes and set the ball down outside the door that the boy had disappeared through.

Even from the next alley over, Roma could still hear the postman grumbling with complaints, an unending stream of thoughts sent out into the open.

Roma stopped. He swiveled on his heel.

Wait a minute.

How was it possible to hunt down one girl out in the rural countryside, among all the many houses and swaths of fields? How was it possible to narrow anything down, especially when people stayed in their own towns and communication moved at a snail's pace?

Well, all you needed was to ask a postman.

Roma barged in through the front door. There was already a commotion going on in the living room, though he wasn't surprised when he realized it was Juliette directing Mila around in a step-by-step drill for an offensive attack, using Yulun for practice while Yulun darted left and right in terror. Mila looked like she was having fun—in comparison to her catatonic response earlier, at least. When her eyes crinkled, she resembled Alisa so fiercely that Roma had to do a double-take, trying to make sense of the dissonance in his head. Logically, he was aware that this was not his sister. The shock did not lessen each time.

"Hello, my love," Juliette called. "Has Ah Tou arrived?"

"He's clearing the alley as we speak," Roma replied. "Should you be doing that before you've disinfected your injuries?"

"I'm teaching Mila how to stab any man retrieving her. More important than disinfection."

Roma tutted, going over and forcibly directing Juliette to sit down before he had an aneurysm. Then he turned to Mila and Yulun.

"I have a question for you both," he said. "Are your names registered in the postal system?"

Yulun furrowed his brow. Mila set the knife in her hand down, tilting her head.

"Yulun is, but I am not," she said. "There's no one to send me letters."

A beat passed.

"Wait, wait, that's not entirely true," Yulun countered, visibly jolting as a thought occurred to him. "Our marriage license required an address. We're in the system together even if you aren't registered."

There it was.

"And every time you fled after Mr. Pyotr's threats," Roma said to Yulun slowly, "I'm sure you wrote letters to your mother from your new residence, yes? I imagine you wanted to keep in contact with her so she didn't worry."

How the two girls in Shanghai had been found was child's play.

The city talked incessantly, and showgirls commandeered attention. Ask around enough, and someone had to know someone who knew the girl you were looking for. The two outside Suzhou must have been a tougher case, but still, anyone who lived near a city must have a job, and anyone who held a job had a circle of people who could be traced.

It was only Mila who made no sense. Middle-of-nowhere township, interacting with no one but her fiancé. So to hunt her down, you had to start with her name in the rural community system. Find a chatty postman who could browse through the records. Mr. Pyotr was getting their exact address somehow; other mercenaries were searching their wider areas somehow.

"Should I not have been writing letters?" Yulun asked hesitantly.

"You couldn't have known," Juliette replied, already following Roma's logic. She tapped her chin. "But if this is how you're being found . . ."

"Maybe we can use it to our advantage," Roma finished, "and draw out some answers."

11

A week passed. As soon as they settled on their plan, Yulun had gone to the nearest postal office that serviced Zhouzhuang and changed his address to Roma and Juliette's. Or rather, he had added his name under Mai Luomin and Mai Zhuli, because Roma and Juliette were a bit more experienced at the art of concealment and were obviously not using their real names.

After the official change, Juliette had poked her head around to Mrs. Fan's house, prepared to sweet-talk the old lady into letting Yulun and Mila stay in her spare room. Juliette had barely finished giving her proposal before Mrs. Fan was bustling around excitedly to prepare for her guests. Mrs. Fan loved company, and putting the two right next door meant Juliette wasn't hovering all the time but, between organizing shipments and calling contacts, she could still poke her head over in the afternoons to keep teaching Mila vital skills—such as flipping a knife in midair.

There probably wasn't much practical use to such a skill, but Juliette was a big believer in instilling confidence. It was impossible to lack confidence once one mastered a knife flip.

"I must head back," she said now, gathering up the box of practice batons they had been using. Dusk was drawing close, as were a multitude of dark clouds low on the horizon. She suppressed a shiver, watching the ripples in the canal pick up speed. "Roma is going to burn down the kitchen if I don't go take over."

A small giggle slipped out of Mila. She was more reserved than Yulun was, but every so often she would take Juliette by surprise, cracking a dirty joke or kicking especially hard when she was mimicking a defensive maneuver. Yulun was fonder of begging off, choosing to sit nearby with a book and shout encouragements instead, but Mila took every opportunity to learn how to protect herself.

"Juliette," Mila said quietly, drawing her attention just before she could go. "Do you think more people are going to come soon?"

People sent by the facility, she meant.

"Maybe," Juliette answered honestly. "But you don't have to worry. Roma and I will be diligently on guard."

Mila hesitated. "But," she said, her voice turning even more quiet. Over by the tree, Yulun hadn't caught the conversation and still had his nose in his book. "What if they're too strong? What if I tear my own throat out?"

"You won't," Juliette said firmly. Allowing no room for argument, she put her hands on the girl's shoulders and gave her a hefty shake. Mila's eyes grew wide, but she didn't protest the aggressive gesture. "I promise you that you won't. We are going to figure out how to keep you safe, and then you and Yulun are going to live in peace, do you understand me?"

Mila nodded. Juliette nodded back, fierce and determined. This world had broken too much; she wasn't going to let it break this. She would take up arms against it herself if it meant another hopeful love saved.

"Go inside now before it gets dark." She raised her voice, waving at Yulun. "I'm off, Yulun!"

The boy waved back from the tree, hopping to his feet. Juliette circled around Mrs. Fan's house and crossed the bridge, shivering again as the sun descended properly. When she opened the door, there was the sound of a pot being moved around in the kitchen, though Juliette headed straight for the bedroom, huffing air onto her fingers to warm them.

She opened the closet. Her favorite white scarf was lurking in here somewhere. The last time she had rummaged around, it had been in the back with her shoes and diamonds. The weather was certainly turning chilly enough to bring it back out.

"Roma?" she called. "Dearest husband of mine, I seek thy aid."

He appeared in the bedroom doorway, wearing an apron. "I am thine to command."

Juliette flashed a coquettish smile. "Where is my—"

"White scarf is on the rack in the washroom. I cleaned it so that it doesn't smell like dust when it starts getting cold."

She mimed a kiss in his direction and hurried into the washroom at the end of the hallway to reunite with her white scarf.

"Stay put," Roma said when she grabbed it off the rack. Something clattered from the bedroom: he had pulled the medicine box off the shelves. "While you're there, your bandages need changing."

That bullet graze on her shoulder had been much worse than expected when they finally cleaned it, crusting angry and red. Roma had been so pale while dabbing at the wound that she thought he might faint entirely. Though Juliette had teased him about forgetting how to dress wounds, at least that meant neither of them *had* dressed a wound in a while.

Roma came into the washroom. He put the box down and gestured for her to turn around, undoing the buttons at her collar.

"It looks to be healing nicely," he remarked when he pulled the old bandage off. He dropped the reddened gauze into the sink.

Juliette craned to look, one hand still clutching her scarf and the other holding her qipao up at the front. "Will it leave a scar?"

"Probably not." Roma opened a bottle of antiseptic. He set the cap down on the sink edge.

"Good. I wouldn't want to offend you by putting a new one over yours."

A wince. He was rather sensitive about the time he had thrown a knife at her.

"Stop teasing," he muttered. "I am very unhappy about each scar you pick up."

Juliette softened. For her, a scar here and there was a rare occasion nowadays, and more likely to be the result of her getting too overzealous with her cooking. The only person in the world who might be protected forever from scars was Rosalind—immortal, unaging Rosalind—but even she was carrying terrible ones from the past.

The thought of her cousin brought a sigh to Juliette's lips. Through the mirror, she caught Roma's gaze flickering up as he secured the bandage, asking without words what was on her mind.

"I have been thinking," Juliette began. "What are we to do if nothing comes of our plan?"

"You mean if no attackers come find Mila here?" Roma pulled her qipao up. "Isn't that a good thing?"

"It is good for her safety, yes." Juliette lowered her arms, letting him fasten her collar again. "But much as I would like to, we cannot look after her indefinitely. She's her own person. We need to let her go sooner or later."

Her qipao latched into place. Roma smoothed his hands along her shoulders, carefully avoiding her injury.

"You sound conflicted," he remarked.

Juliette sighed again. It was a colossal sound. "Because if it comes to letting her go, then I feel like we've failed. I want us to maintain our safety, protect our identities. But I also want us to do what is right. And one cannot be wholly realized without the other, because the more we play hero, the larger the targets grow on our backs."

They could use their contacts, issue a region-wide proclamation to demand Milyena be left alone. But then it would rub up against the wrong people, and someone would go digging, and if their identities came into the open . . .

Roma smoothed his hand along her back now, as if he were trying to smooth away the imaginary targets that Juliette had dreamt up.

"I know, dorogaya," he said lowly. "We will walk this balancing act for the rest of time. The life we chose is a perpetual tightrope."

It twisted at her heart to hear aloud. She would do it all again if she could. She would take all the same steps—relive every agonizing moment and accept every old wound—if it meant this future here. But she was so intensely aware that this life of hers was a self-regarding one; each day that passed, it was her and Roma choosing themselves over the world. At what point did it turn them rotten? How many times did they need to wave off the cries knocking at their door before they became hardened to the humanity that used to make their whole world?

"I suppose I wonder sometimes," she said, "how it would look if we swayed on the tightrope a little more."

She looked into the mirror to her side. Watched him.

"You mean if we didn't focus so much on hiding," Roma clarified. "Is that terrible?"

"Of course not." The set of Roma's brow softened. "We didn't actually come out here to hide, darling Juliette. We came here to live. If hiding is what brings us the safety to do so, then we abide by it. If a day comes when we cannot reconcile our intention to live with hiding anymore, then we shed some of our acquired mystique appropriately. We don't need to make up our minds right this moment."

Juliette couldn't quite fill her lungs. She didn't know if it was because of the terrifying thought of emerging from their safety, or

·because Roma speaking in his sense of grandeur always took her breath away a little.

"You make it sound so easy."

"Why can't it be?"

She turned around properly, facing him. Time brushed up against her cheek and asked her to take a breath, but she only held still, reveling in the swirl of emotion shaking through her ribs. Her heart turned itself inside out, read aloud the writing in red on her arteries and valves, told her pointedly that love was never wholly the grand battles and explosive deeds. *Love*, she thought, was that kernel of warmth nestled deeper in her chest, glowing with a sense of comfort whenever Roma's eyes were on her—the same comfort she'd first found when they were fifteen, everlasting.

Juliette put her scarf on the sink edge. She stretched her arms out. "Come closer, please?"

He obliged.

A breath in. A breath out. Her nose pressed into his neck and his cheek leaning against her head.

"Hey," Juliette said. The word was muffled because she hadn't bothered drawing away first.

"Hmm?"

"We should have a fight."

Roma made a perplexed sound, thinking he had misheard her. "I beg your pardon?"

"We're too content with each other all the time," she continued. "It's unnatural."

A pause. Then Roma spluttered with laughter, his whole body shaking with the absurdity of her statement. Juliette pulled back to scowl at him, and he only laughed harder.

"It is very much not," he countered firmly when he had gotten ahold of himself. "The scales tipped too far when we were younger. This is a slow restoration of justice."

"And at what point are the scales entirely restored?"

"Never." In a sudden swoop, Roma employed his favorite tactic, grabbing her by the waist and picking her up to the sound of her squeal. "You are stuck with me and utter contentment for all of time and beyond."

The next day, Juliette took her shopping basket to the open market. She wandered around the fish at a leisurely pace, peering at each display before finally pointing to a smaller one at the back, waiting for the stall owner to wrap it up and weigh the catch.

The fall season was fully shedding its skin. Though the weeping willows that leaned over the canals would stay green year-round, they were thinning significantly, leaves dropping into the water and running along the currents like miniature canoes. Juliette walked home with her basket swinging, watching the blue sky deepen into the color of high noon.

She hadn't been planning to stop by Mrs. Fan's house, but as she passed by, her elderly neighbor poked her head out the window.

"Mai tàitài, I saw the postman knocking at your door before. He set your mail on the front stoop."

"Oh?" she said, pausing outside Mrs. Fan's window. "My husband has been home all morning."

"To be very fair, he knocked for less than a few seconds before setting off."

Juliette shook her head. Classic. "I will fetch it. Yulun and Mila are well?"

"They are dearies. Come over for dinner tonight. I am making hóngshāo ròu."

"How could I possibly say no to that?" Juliette resumed walking, stepping onto the bridge to cross the canal. "See you soon, Fan nǎinai."

Juliette trekked to the other side, walking the thin path to the front door carefully, then bending over to pick up the mail on the stoop. The envelopes looked like the usual reports they got from their eyes in the city. Jiemin liked sending letters instead of making phone calls. He claimed it was harder to get caught when he was mostly working undercover for the Nationalists.

Juliette pushed through the door. Inside, Roma was sitting at the desk, a beam of sunlight shining against the side of his face while he concentrated on a balance sheet.

"Hello, my love."

Roma silently inclined his cheek toward her without taking his eyes away from his math, asking for a greeting kiss. Juliette leaned in, making a dramatic sound upon contact.

"Oh my goodness," Roma complained, jolting in his seat. "That was such a wet kiss."

"It is your punishment." She set the basket and envelopes down, then perched on the edge of the desk so that she was facing him. "Not even a hello for your own wife. Have you no shame?"

He dropped his pen, grabbed her wrists, and pulled her onto his lap, his attention fixed on her properly now.

"Stop trying to pick a fight," he said. When he leaned closer, his breath was hot against her jaw. "I see right through your trickster ways."

"Just one fight," Juliette returned, accepting that she had been caught out. "You love screaming at me."

"Lies." A glint appeared in his eye. He seemed to consider it briefly, if for no other reason than to amuse themselves through the day, but then his gaze moved to what she had brought in.

Juliette looked at the envelopes too. "They got left outside."

"Messages from the city, I'm assuming?" he asked. While Juliette hopped off his lap, taking the shopping basket and putting its contents into the kitchen, Roma reached for the envelopes. Flipped through them.

"Juliette, what is this?"

He held up one of the envelopes. A fish clutched in her hands, Juliette turned around in curiosity.

The front of the envelope was entirely blank. Juliette hastened over again, still gripping the fish.

"Open it."

"There is a fish in my face, dorogaya."

"Ignore the fish and open it."

Roma opened the envelope. Out fluttered a slip of paper, penned in Russian.

I told you there would be consequences. I am the only one who can help you now.

For a long moment, Juliette and Roma both stared at the words, uncomprehending. The moment that Roma shouted aloud, Juliette pivoted fast too, hurrying to set the fish into the icebox in the kitchen, washing her hands and shaking water everywhere.

They had been waiting for more hired men to show up, hopeful that they could garner some answers and stop the facility from coming after Mila. But this address change had summoned Mr. Pyotr directly.

"It's only two o'clock," Juliette exclaimed. "The postman is most definitely still in the area. He must have *some* firm answer on where this envelope came from, or else he wouldn't have known to deliver it here."

Roma reached under the desk, pulling free a knife taped to the base and handing it to her. Juliette blinked. She had forgotten it was there. Far too many weapons were taped in the strangest places around the house.

"Here. You take the route along the western canal. I'll circle through the north."

"What is our signal if we find the postman?" She accepted the knife.

"It's only the postman. Shout really loudly."

Juliette harrumphed. "Zhouzhuang isn't *that* small."

"It will work. Come on, we're burning daylight."

Roma pulled the door open, patting his pockets to check for weapons. With a grumble, Juliette hurried up behind him, propping her hands on his shoulders and leaning close to his ear.

"I'm going to count this as an argument."

"That was a mild disagreement and some cajoling on my end *at best*." He craned his head back, giving her a short kiss. "But I will let you say so if it pleases you."

Roma hurried off.

"Stop pleasing me so much!" Juliette yelled after him.

"I can't help it, you're the love of my life!" Roma shouted back. "Meet at the main road if you find the postman!"

He disappeared over the bridge. Fighting back an embarrassing little smile, Juliette pulled their front door firmly shut, crossed the bridge, and set off in the other direction.

Roma kept his pace natural, not wanting to incite any suspicion while he sought his target. He doubted the postman was responsible for any of these events, but one could never be too careful.

"Mr. Mai, I haven't seen you in days."

Right before Roma could pass by the flower shop, the owner inside gestured for him to come in. He could hardly say no. Besides, maybe the owner could help.

Roma ducked under the low-hanging wind chimes. The shop fronts by the main canals were stout, cramped spaces. The flower shop barely had room for two shelves on either side holding up its bouquets, with a register in the middle to conduct business.

"Sheng lǎo ye," Roma greeted. "I don't suppose you have seen the postman come through?"

Mr. Sheng pulled his white beard, deep in thought. He sprinkled some water over the nearest bouquets. "The postman? I don't think he has been around yet. I am waiting for money from my son. I would know if it had arrived."

Which meant that maybe the postman was still somewhere south of here.

Excellent.

"Let me know if he comes by, would you?" Roma asked. He pointed to a small bundle of red roses. "Also, I will have that."

A few coins lighter and a rose bouquet acquired, Roma proceeded down the canal again, keeping his head forward this time to avoid being summoned by any more elderly shopkeepers looking for company. Try as he did to stay focused on his search, he had barely proceeded onto the next turn when he almost collided with Mrs. Ding, who ran the fish stall at the markets.

"Hello, lad," she said. "What are you in such a rush for?"

Roma looked at the flowers in his hand.

"It's my wife's birthday," he lied on the spot. "The postman was supposed to bring a gift today, but he is taking far too long to arrive. Have you seen him?"

"Sure." Mrs. Ding pointed behind her. "He was at the Plum Blossom Teahouse just then."

"Ding tàitài, you are a blessing to the world." He sidled past her on the thin walkway. "I will be bringing gifts for you tomorrow too."

The Plum Blossom Teahouse was two left turns and one canal away. This time he really did need to ignore the two elderly women who called out from their stores, then the clump of kids playing a marble game. Roma paused for the barest moment, nostalgic at the very sight, but he forced himself back on task.

He ran off the last bridge he crossed. Came to a pause a few feet away from the Plum Blossom Teahouse, then watched the postman step off its front ledge, waving goodbye to the hostess he had been chatting with.

Roma picked up his pace. With his eyes pinned on the postman, he followed him for a considerable few seconds, taking inventory of their surroundings. It wasn't until they passed an offshoot path— one which led toward the back doors of several shops—that Roma lunged forward and grabbed the postman's collar with his left hand, shoving him into the path and slamming him hard into the wall. His post bag full of letters made a dense *thwack!* against the bricks.

"Don't yell," Roma warned immediately. "Sometime this morning, you made a delivery for the house by the outermost canal in Zhouzhuang. Next to the large weeping willow tree. Do you remember?"

The postman was trembling under Roma's hold. This was a different worker from the man who had been delivering around the main canals last week, younger. Juliette usually collected their mail, so Roma didn't know if this man was new or if he just hadn't paid enough attention to the usual faces bringing their envelopes.

"Y-yes, I remember."

"Good," Roma said. "Then do you remember what you delivered? There was a blank envelope mixed in there. Why did you put it with the others?"

The postman's lip wobbled. Roma waited, counting to three in his head before shaking the man's collar, and he relented immediately.

"I was asked! Someone gave me the envelope just before I left the post office at dawn." The postman flinched, trying to press his head into the wall to get away. "He . . . he looked a little like you, actually. Slightly foreign. Spoke Chinese well, though."

"Russian accent?" Roma confirmed.

"I—I would wager yes. Stronger than yours. You don't have one."

"Yes, well, I was born here." Roma let go of the postman. He pondered for a moment. "Do you have any idea who he was?"

The postman swallowed hard. Though he had been released, he didn't move, as if he were afraid Roma might attack again on the slightest provocation. Roma hadn't even grabbed him that hard to begin with.

"I don't know. B-but, uh, he has been to the post office enough times that I did recognize his face. Actually, one moment . . ."

Eagerly, he plunged a hand into his bag, sifting through a large wad of envelopes. Roma watched him search, eyeing each stamped corner he flipped through until he brought one out.

"Here—his return address, on the back. I think this is merely a shopping catalogue order, so he gave them to me together."

Roma plucked the envelope from the postman's hand, flipping it over fast. The address wasn't far from here. A short drive.

"I hope there are no hard feelings," Roma said, clapping the postman on the shoulder. The postman recoiled with fright, but Roma was already running for the main road, an envelope in one hand and the bouquet of roses still in the other.

Juliette was waiting by the road, leaning up against the township's main gate. Her eyes widened when she saw him approach, taking in his disheveled appearance.

"You found him?"

"Get in the car," Roma instructed in answer, tipping his chin toward the gravel lot beyond the gate, where their vehicle was parked. "We have an address. Oh, and . . ." He gave her the flowers. "These are for you."

12

"How do we want to do this?"

Juliette was busy burying her face in the flowers, inhaling the sweet scent. "Guns blazing?"

Roma gave her a wry look. After a forty-five-minute drive, they had arrived at their destination, close to Suzhou. A train rumbled nearby, loudly enough that it vibrated the paved roads. He put the car in park, the two of them peering out the windshield at the town streets.

"How do we want to do this *before* the guns come out?"

Juliette hummed in thought. She slid her hand along his arm, squeezing once. "I will do the shooting if you want, my love."

Before Roma could protest, she set her flowers down gently, then hopped out of the car, smoothing her hair back. Roma followed suit quickly, closing his car door.

"Here is another idea," he said. "We pretend to be solicitors. He invites us in; we confirm if it is Mr. Pyotr."

"What are we soliciting?" Juliette asked. They started to walk. The house—the apartment, really, on closer inspection—was located at the end of the street, tucked between what looked to be two drugstores. It was all one building, the middle spliced out for a single-level segment with a green front door.

"Funds for medical research." Roma reached his hand out. "That will get his attention."

"All right. I like that." She took his offered hand, fingers interlacing. "And *then* the guns start blazing?"

Roma sighed with affection and exasperation in equal measure. "You," he muttered, "are such a pain in the ass."

Juliette sidled closer. "I could *really* be a pain in your ass—"

"That was absolutely not an invitation to begin wheedling me about your infernal agenda again."

"Roma. Do consider it. Other men have said—"

"Shhh . . . I'm knocking."

They released each other, then straightened their postures and smoothed their expressions out. Roma's knuckles thudded against the painted green surface.

When the man on the other side opened the door, it was certainly someone who matched Mr. Pyotr's description. He eyed them curiously, hand gripping the frame.

"Do you have a moment?" Juliette started in Russian. She smiled brightly when the possible Mr. Pyotr blinked in surprise. "Sources have sent us your way to canvass for help."

"We have come from a rural hospital for immigrants," Roma continued. "There's a proposal underway, and we would love for you to be a sponsor. Might we come in?"

Before they could be denied, Roma stepped over the threshold, firmly inviting himself into the apartment. Juliette pressed down on her urge to smirk, biting her tongue as she hurried to follow. There was only one window inside, on the far wall. Understandably, the afternoon sunlight was having a difficult time seeping through, the corners of the living room lurking dark and gloomy.

Juliette paused by a framed diploma hanging on the wall. PYOTR GAVRILOVICH SPIKOV.

They had found the right man. She inclined her head toward the certificate, directing Roma's attention over.

"What is this about?" Pyotr Gavrilovich said. He hurried to close the door, his brows knitting together. Patches of silver threaded through his hair at the sides, which Juliette had to guess put his age in his late thirties. He had a calendar propped next to an empty vase on the table. The month was prematurely turned to November.

"Let me tell you about some of the hospital's history," Roma started. Taking a seat on one of the armrests on the couch, Roma launched into complete make-believe, which was something he had gotten better at over the years after realizing that if he left the make-believe to Juliette, she would often go too far and get caught too early. She was rather prone to exaggeration. Juliette could admit that about herself.

Meanwhile, she stayed standing, making a slow perusal of what she could discern about the apartment. One pair of shoes by the door. Bare walls save for the diploma. In the kitchen, which was separated by a divider, a single dirty bowl stained the table. In the bedroom, only an unmade bed occupied the space.

The most interesting matter, however, was the bookshelf next to the bedroom door. A miniature safe sat on the top shelf, its small door swung open.

There were two vials inside, containing a clear liquid. Both were half filled and plugged with a stopper.

Juliette must have made a noise or started toward the discovery, because Pyotr quickly shuffled in the bookshelf's direction. Though Roma was still talking, his words started to slow as Pyotr's attention grew distracted, coming to a complete stop when the man reached for the safe and slammed its door shut, the echo reverberating loudly into the apartment.

Abrupt silence.

Juliette tilted her head. "Is there a problem?"

"Problem?" Pyotr echoed. "Of course not."

"That's a shame." Juliette reached inside her qipao skirt. "Because *I* have a problem. And I thought you offered your help."

She leveled her gun at him. A moment passed while the scientist stared at her in shock, digesting the turn of conversation and the weapon pointed in his direction. Then his hands flew up, palms outward in plea.

"Please be sensible about this," he said calmly. "There is no reason to point your gun at me."

Roma dropped his nice demeanor. "She never needs a reason to point her gun anyway. Hands on your head, away from your clothes."

Pyotr followed the instructions slowly. Though he had his palms out, they had been very close to his jacket pocket, as if he had been about to reach for a weapon.

"I have some very simple questions." Juliette wandered closer. "Let's start with why you're here. Why are you following Mila?"

From behind, Roma came to stand at her side, his arms crossed. Pyotr's eyes flickered once more, eyeing his possibility of escape.

"I can answer your questions—please watch the trigger," he said calmly. "I am a scientist. I am here for my research, not to harm Milyena."

"And yet all four of her friends are dead," Roma cut in.

"That is not my fault," Pyotr shot back. "I split from the research facility because of a difference in opinion. They didn't think it a big deal when our first batch of experiments fled. Very well—I swallowed my concerns, even if I didn't think we could replicate the same findings."

"What findings?" Roma interrupted. "Brainwashing?"

Pyotr hesitated. "If you need to call it that, I suppose so. A better term is chemical conditioning. It had never been done before. It wasn't easy to get the right conditions. So the board didn't like that our second group failed, demanded we keep studying and studying to no avail. Then they blamed me when it was the first group's information they wanted after all, three years after the fact."

Juliette watched his expression very carefully. He looked like he was telling the truth. The timing matched up too.

"Then you came down to get them back."

"*No*," Pyotr replied. "I told you: I split. The board members are obviously the ones coming after her. All I want is my research. I tried to warn Milyena. I am the only one who can help her."

"Wait a second." Roma did a little circle on his heel. He perched on the armrest again, looking effortlessly casual while Juliette held the weapon. "Why are you after your own research? Did you not already possess it *before* experimenting on the girls?"

Pyotr hesitated. Juliette narrowed her eyes.

"It wasn't your research," she said, making the guess before he spoke. "It was Lourens's."

At once, Pyotr's attention snapped up in shock. "How do you know Lourens?"

Juliette frowned, waving her gun. "I am asking the questions. What was it, then? You stole his research, gave it to the girls? He found out and decided to leave?"

"Look, how about this?" Pyotr used his chin to gesture at one of the low tables beside the couch, directing Roma's attention over while Juliette kept her eyes pinned on him. "There is paper and pen over there. I know where Lourens is, so I can give you his address. Go to him, and he will have the answers you seek."

"I would rather like Lourens's location. . . ." Roma made his way to the table, then tugged open its single drawer and retrieved a sheet of paper. "However, that doesn't get you off the hook. Why are you the only one who can help Mila?"

Pyotr looked like he was barely stopping himself from straining forward. He had some plan up his sleeve—Juliette could smell it. But she allowed it to unfold. She was rather curious what he wanted to try.

"Answer the question," Juliette prompted.

Roma found the pen in the drawer. He didn't bring it to Pyotr yet. He held on to it. And Pyotr exhaled tightly, saying, "Lourens and I worked *together*. Maybe he invented most of the chemical conditioning, but I contributed work too. Critical work."

Juliette and Roma exchanged a glance. Equal wariness passed back and forth.

"Well?" Juliette said. "What sort?"

Pyotr swallowed hard. "The details are too complex."

"I don't believe you in any fashion."

"I am here to pursue knowledge," Pyotr seethed. "At every end it is only others trying to take it away—"

"So did Lourens take something from you?"

"I did not say that—"

"Then you took something from Lourens," Roma cut in.

Pyotr was turning red in the face. "How dare you say such—*enough*. I am here to help. *I am the only one who can help Milyena.*"

"And help yourself in the process, I'm sure." Juliette brought the gun closer until it pressed right against Pyotr's temple. She tilted her head, watching him. He narrowed his eyes in return, and narrowed them even further when she asked: "Were you in Shanghai during the madness?"

"No," Pyotr snapped.

"Funny," Roma followed immediately. "You didn't even ask what the madness was. You would think someone from Vladivostok might show a bit of confusion."

A flash of something passed behind Pyotr's gaze. It didn't matter whether he was lying or not. Maybe he had been present in Shanghai and had witnessed it himself. But if he hadn't, then he showed no confusion because he had heard about its details from Lourens. If he claimed to be the only one who could help Mila, then he had been inspired by the tales of madness and was the very one who had put this mechanism in place.

Roma walked forward at last.

"Here." He put the pen and paper down. "*Slowly*. I want Lourens's full location—no detail-skimping on the street name or suburb."

Following instructions, Pyotr moved his hands away from his head carefully. "I am going to pick up the pen now." He picked up the pen. Pressed the nib to the paper and started to write, providing an address in Vladivostok. "I'm putting the pen down now."

He reached for the other end of the pen, looking like he was going to secure the ink nib.

Instead, when the pen turned, a blade flicked out, and Pyotr shoved forward.

Juliette caught his wrist, rolling her eyes. Was that it? The whole plan that had been whirling behind his eyes while he talked? She twisted his arm hard, and Pyotr yelled out, dropping the pen. It clattered to the floor. Roma glanced down to track where it was rolling, his nose scrunched like he smelled something bad.

"You could have at least lunged for me instead," he said dully. "My reflexes are a little slower."

"Enough," Pyotr spat. He yanked his arm free from Juliette's hold, then was forced to freeze immediately when her gun pressed to his forehead again. "I have done nothing wrong. Let me go."

Juliette laughed humorlessly. "You gave five girls ticking time bombs inside their own bodies," she said, "and you say you did nothing wrong? Four of them are *dead*."

Pyotr's eyes flickered in the direction of the safe again.

"It is a matter of protection," he argued. He didn't deny Juliette's accusation. "Lourens did not do the work alone. Those are my findings too. My right to claim, not the board's. They think they can pay their dirty money and fix their mistakes—*they* allowed the first set of girls to leave. No one would be dead if the board had only listened to me. If they want to steal my research, all they will get are corpses. The moment they try to take blood to study, all they will get are *corpses*."

Juliette felt slathered in disgust. An image of those vials inside the safe flashed in her head, then the memory of what the man in the alley had said: *We are doing our damn best to knock them out and keep them unharmed. . . . They are brainwashed to kill themselves the moment we get near.*

It wasn't proximity. The hired men had misunderstood, had probably repeatedly triggered the mechanism by not noticing what was really causing the faux madness: a needle to the skin. A preventative measure so that no one could ever commence research without killing the subject entirely. Something as simple as trying to sedate the girls would likely have the same effect.

"You seem to be telling me that you have no desire to fix Mila," Juliette observed.

Pyotr made a noise under his breath, seeming to realize that he had gone too far and said too much. "That's untrue."

Roma kicked the pen away from where it had landed on the floor. Then he walked up to the bookshelf, staring at the miniature safe.

"If she's kept brainwashed forever, though, it means you can order her around *and* no one else can study her." Roma pointed at the safe. "What is in here?"

He, too, had noticed that Pyotr's attention kept drifting over.

"Research," Pyotr answered tightly.

"What sort?" Roma demanded. "Because this is Lourens's safe."

Pyotr blinked. Some of his anger transformed into sheer incomprehension. "Who *are* you people?"

"The wrong people to be upsetting." Juliette was at the end of her patience. "We won't ask so nicely again. *What is in there?*"

His lip curled with a sneer.

"A reset mixture," he finally spat. "When injected, it targets each chemical instruction given to a subject and erases what has been put into place."

Juliette's breath snagged. In other words, it was a cure. The simplest solution to fix Mila, and he merely kept it away, waiting for these people to come after her and unknowingly cause her death.

"Open it."

"No," Pyotr declared. Triumph settled into his manner. "I won't. And you must put that gun away, because you cannot kill me or else the safe's combination dies with me, and you will *never* fix that girl."

The apartment fell quiet. Roma and Juliette exchanged another glance, communicating a decision. In the aftermath of his declaration, Pyotr looked very, very smug.

Then Juliette fired her gun.

The bullet embedded right into the man's forehead. Blood sprayed, red as rubies, and Pyotr fell backward with a thud, landing on his carpet at an awkward angle before stilling. Dead.

"God," she said, wiping the spatter from her neck, "he was so annoying. Does he think safes are bulletproof?"

Roma grimaced, shuffling back before the spreading puddle of blood on the carpet could touch his shoes. "Juliette . . ."

"Don't worry, don't worry," she assured, stepping away from the puddle too. "I came prepared."

She patted her qipao and found the invoice she had been carrying around. A statement showing a high amount of money owed. She slapped it on the table and positioned it so that it could be easily spotted by anyone who walked through the door. The authorities were going to think this was a debt killing. Hopefully the rumors would spread back to the weapons ring operating out of Zhouzhuang. Two birds with one stone: a nasty elimination and their reputation aided.

Roma grabbed the safe, lugging it down from the top shelf.

Curiously, he peered over the table while he walked a few steps, reading the invoice. "How long have you been carrying that around?"

"Too long. Put the safe down."

Compliantly, Roma set the safe on the floor a distance away from the body. "One moment." He stepped back, fingers plugged into his ears. "All right. Go on."

Juliette shot at the lock. She emptied out the round in her gun, crouching down to peer at the damage. It looked as if a few more would do the trick.

She turned to Roma. "My love?"

He handed her his pistol without further prompting. Juliette aimed, and the next bullet tore the lock clean off, the door slowly creaking open.

Juliette snatched out the two vials.

"We can run some tests, I am sure," Roma was saying as they got out of the car. He held the vials up to the early evening light. Something in the clear liquid was glinting each time it caught the orange sun.

"Tomorrow," Juliette decided, visibly holding back a yawn. They stepped through Zhouzhuang's main gate, trudging into one of its smaller paths. "We have one threat eliminated, so there's no need to rush—"

She swiveled suddenly. Roma followed her line of sight, concerned as he put the vials away.

"What is it?" he asked. He could smell dinner from one of these houses, wafting out into the air.

"I thought I saw someone running past in that other alley," Juliette answered. "I got a terrible chill."

Roma didn't know if he was simply too readily prepared to switch his demeanor the moment Juliette was on alert, but a shudder ran down his spine in an instant. He reached for her arm, pushing them forward. "Let's get home. It's eerie at this hour."

They walked fast. Doors in the alleys blew open and slammed closed. Teahouse staff threw buckets of water out onto the streets. The canals ran and ran and ran.

One street away from their house, Juliette stopped short again. This time, Roma fully expected something to barge out from the shadows and looked around before he even asked what was wrong.

"Look, I know we're both out of bullets, but if we hold our guns up threateningly . . ."

"Wait, Roma," Juliette whispered. "Listen."

It was Mrs. Fan's shouting.

Juliette raced forward. Roma was close behind. He made a rapid scan of the outside of Mrs. Fan's house, at first finding nothing out of the ordinary. Then he caught sight of a single shard of glass on the pathway from a half-broken window, and he drew his empty gun.

"Fan nǎinai?" Juliette yelled, kicking through the front door.

When Roma followed, the two of them charged into the room as smoothly as a zip parting along the middle. Juliette picked up a cup on the table and hurled it fast at the man lunging for Mrs. Fan; Roma raised his pistol at the man who had already gotten ahold of Mila, forcing him to freeze with one hand around her arm. She looked terrified. Her knuckles were bright pink, as if she had tried to fend them off. At the other side of the room, Yulun had a broomstick in his hands, raised in preparation, though he was shaking.

Both of the intruders had angels tattooed to the sides of their necks.

"Release her," Roma commanded. He walked a step closer to the man. "Now."

The other mercenary slumped to the floor. Juliette had thrown the cup hard enough to smash into shards between his eyes, knocking him out.

"Calm down," the first man said. A syringe appeared in his other hand. "I am not here to retrieve her. I have only been told to collect a vial of blood for research. Then I will let her go, and we are all happy."

"No, stop!" Juliette called. Extreme alarm filled her tone. "You don't understand—"

The mercenary pricked the needle into Mila's arm.

As soon as the needle touched her, Mila screamed and hurled herself away with unnatural strength.

Then her hands flew to her throat.

Roma was flooded with memory at once, standing stock-still in the room, unable to move. Alisa. The very same madness had infected Alisa that first time and she had tried to claw out her own throat, and Roma hadn't been able to *help* her—

"Yulun!" Juliette shouted. "Give me that damn broomstick!"

With a cry of fright, Yulun threw her the broomstick just as she was running forward, and with barely any pause in her movement, she smashed it hard on the mercenary's head. At last, Roma snapped out of his stupor, lunging for Mila and trying to tear her hands away.

"Mila, Mila!" he yelled as blood streamed down her neck. "You're going to be fine. Hold on! Just hold on!"

Juliette abandoned the broomstick as soon as the mercenary went down, tossing it to the floor and scanning the space around him. As Roma used his whole strength to keep Mila's hands still, he couldn't see what Juliette was doing—not until he turned, prepared to shout for some rope so they could tie Mila down, and he caught sight of her lunging for the dropped syringe.

They were taking the risk, then.

"Roma!"

"It's in my pocket!"

She scrambled to retrieve one of the vials. Tore the stopper out, then stuck the needle into the liquid, filling its whole barrel. Just as Mila was about to claw right into muscle, Juliette stabbed the needle into her arm and plunged down.

Immediately, Mila went limp.

A whimper sounded in the room. Yulun.

Slowly, Roma released his tight grip on Mila's wrists. Her hands had stopped fighting him. Her eyes were glazed over. Yulun ran forward, coming to a stop before her.

"Mila?" he whispered. "Mila, are you okay?"

Mila stayed silent. Staring. At her other side, Juliette sat down on the floor with a sudden thump, looking ready to cry. Mrs. Fan hurried to her, hunching down to pat her shoulder.

"You did your best," Mrs. Fan whispered.

"*Mila*," Yulun called again. He tapped her face repeatedly. "Please, say something."

Roma took a step back. He couldn't watch this a second longer. He couldn't watch if Mila were suddenly to collapse, and with that thought alone, he himself folded down, staggering before Juliette and sinking to his knees.

"Juliette," he said hoarsely. He reached for her hand.

"I can't bear it," she replied, just as quietly. "Not more loss. Not—"

"Yulun?"

Roma's gaze whipped up. Juliette's breath snagged. As Yulun gave Mila another encouraging tap upon her face, Mila blinked rapidly, life returning in the flush of pink rising to her cheeks.

"What happened?" she asked. "I think I lost consciousness."

He felt Juliette tighten her grip on his hand.

"You were going for your throat," Yulun answered shakily, trying to wipe off some of the blood at her chin. "But they got to you in time. Roma and Juliette got to you."

Mila glanced at them. Her hair was tangled. Her eyes were bright.

"I'm . . . I'm not affected by the experiments anymore?"

Juliette sniffled. She was still holding the syringe in her other hand, and Roma took it from her carefully. He rose upright with the unsteadiness of a startled woodland creature, gesturing for Mila to hold her arm out.

"Tell me if there is even the slightest strange feeling, all right?" he said hoarsely.

Mila offered her wrist, still slathered in red. Roma brought the syringe near. Nearer. Its point touched down on skin, then sank in the barest hairsbreadth.

"Nothing?" he asked her.

Mila shook her head. "I don't feel anything."

Roma's breath of relief practically filled the room, stretching from corner to corner. When he turned back to look at Juliette, he caught the single tear tracking down her cheek, but she wiped it before anyone else could see.

"Then you are free," Juliette declared.

13

The fireplace was crackling.

Juliette sat with her legs curled on the sofa, a blanket thrown over her lower half. It had gotten rapidly colder this week, rain pouring hard on the rooftop panels and collecting in large puddles. Before he set out for errands, Roma had built the fire to prevent the entire house from feeling like an icebox. Warmth escaped too easily out of the cracks in old infrastructure, but at least they owned plenty of blankets.

There was a book on her lap. To tell the truth, she hadn't been reading for the last ten minutes, too focused on not dripping persimmon juice everywhere while she munched on the fruit. Yulun had sent a gift basket after they'd settled into a new residence, returning near his mother and her teahouse. The two angel-tattoo mercenaries had also been sent Ah Tou's way. Though they could hope that the facility would be scared into leaving Mila alone after receiving reports of so many failed attempts, there was no way to know. But regardless of whether a new group might show up or if the facility would give up, Mila wanted to return to her regular life. She had been freed of the experiments. She wouldn't be compelled to hurt herself anymore. That was the most important thing.

And if anyone else tried, Mila was also armed and had gotten very good at stabbing.

The rain pummeled on. Juliette finished her fruit. Turned the page. Most of her light was coming from the fireplace, since the day was too gray and groggy. She angled her book over her knee, then grimaced when it shifted her blanket and gave her leg a shock of cold air.

"Oof," she muttered beneath her breath, shivering.

Three rapid knocks sounded on the front door, signaling Roma's return. He stepped in a beat later, collapsing his umbrella and resting it on the coat rack, a newspaper tucked under his arm and a bag filled with roasted chestnuts clutched in his hand.

Roma paused.

"Juliette," he said, his tone flummoxed. "What's the matter?"

She arched an eyebrow. "Nothing. Why would something be the matter?"

He looked around, still hovering by the doorway. "Are you upset? Why are you staying over there?"

"I—what? You knocked three times. Hands full."

Roma set down the bag. Threw over the slightly damp newspaper bundle so that it landed near her feet. "When has that ever stopped you?"

Juliette rolled her eyes, nudging some of her blanket aside. Despite appearances, she was suffused with sheer delight over his lamenting tone. He was such a pampered lover.

"I am merely *cold* and didn't want to get up. Come here and let me steal your body warmth."

Roma shed his jacket. He strode over and dropped down, barely making a word of protest when Juliette stuck her cold hands under his shirt.

"I got the weekly paper from Shanghai," he said, reaching for the bundle. "Toss or read?"

"Read," Juliette replied. "As long as it is not about my parents."

Roma leaned back into the sofa. He started to roll off the rubber band holding the news bundle together, looking concerned. "Was there something concerning recently?"

"No, it's not that." Juliette forced a smile, but it felt artificial on her lips. "They have been appearing a lot, that's all. The more news there is about the civil war, the more frequently they are mentioned to remark on their economic contribution."

A sigh. Roma leaned in and pressed a kiss to her temple. "Are you okay?"

She shrugged. Juliette peered up at him, blowing a breath to get a strand of hair out of her eyes so that her vision wasn't obscured. "Sometimes I get shaken unsteady. It happens. There are two parent-shaped holes in my heart."

Roma reached over to get her hair out of the way. "It *is* quite hard to hold steady all the time with holes in your heart," he agreed quietly. "You will always have the extra pulp of my heart to borrow from, though. It might not fill that space just right, but at least it gives you a place to land on days your balance is weak."

This time, Juliette's smile was real. "Where did you get extra heart pulp from?"

Roma finally finagled the rubber band off. "I started fixing up the holes in my heart from a younger age. It means I have excess to spare these days."

"How fortunate for me." Her arms tightened. "I love you."

"I love you too, dorogaya." The newspaper unfurled. "We really need a place to put these rubber bands because—"

Roma cut himself off suddenly, his jaw going slack. When Juliette followed his gaze and registered the front-page headline, she jolted ten times more vigorously.

LANG SHALIN ALIVE. HONG LIWEN HANJIAN.

"Oh my God," Juliette exclaimed. She clambered upright onto her knees, clutching the newspaper. "Is this today's issue?"

"Fresh from the presses less than an hour ago. This *just* happened."

In awe, Juliette scanned the article, reading the information as fast as she could. Rosalind had aided the arrest of multiple employees working for the Japanese government to incite terror. It had come hand in hand with a conspiracy spearheaded by national traitors in their own government, collaborating with the invading imperial empire.

"This is Rosalind's operation partner," Juliette whispered. "Hong Liwen."

Roma had been reading over her shoulder. "It says he's hanjian."

"It also says he has been taken as a brainwashed soldier of the empire as part of their *chemical experiments*." Juliette rocked back, sitting on the sofa again. "What is going *on*?"

For a long moment, Roma and Juliette kept staring at the newspaper, accompanied only by the sound of wood burning and popping. Then, at once, they seemed to have the same thought, exchanging a gaze and looking into the kitchen where that other vial taken from Pyotr stayed hidden in the cupboard.

"Roma," Juliette said.

"Juliette," he returned.

"We cannot go to her, though. We will be recognized in a heartbeat inside city borders."

Roma's eyes were soft. Warm. "She can come to us."

They had the very item that could help. And heavens knew that with the situation her cousin was currently in, Rosalind needed the help. But . . .

"Are we really going to do this?" Juliette whispered. "Are we going to risk it?"

"I am with you if you want to, and I am with you if you cannot." When Roma reached forward to fold the newspaper up, his ring flashed and caught the firelight, blazing gold. "Ah Cao is coming in ten minutes to take the document shipments. He can also make a phone call from somewhere untraceable. What do you want to do?"

She was so scared. This beautiful life, this tremendous love. It didn't seem fair to have fought so hard for peace only to throw it away.

But she couldn't live with herself if she pretended she never saw this headline. If she let that vial sit in the cupboard forever. She had abandoned Rosalind once already. How could she do it again?

Juliette clambered out of the blanket. "I will write a note," she said breathlessly. "Ah Cao can make the call and pass it on directly."

She closed her hand around a pen. Fetched a blank piece of paper.

I can help you get him back. Find me in Zhouzhuang.

Juliette paused. Looked up. Over on the sofa, Roma was lit like a dark star, surrounded by the glow of the fire and the soft threads of the blankets. She could still stop. Tear up the piece of paper. Protect her peace and her life.

But then Roma gave her an encouraging smile, full of relentless belief. And Juliette steeled herself, because she had him, and that was all that she needed to protect.

She signed off.

—JM.

THIS
FOUL
MURDER

FOR BENEDIKT AND MARSHALL

1

JANUARY 1932

The socks were bundled at the upper left corner, the shirts crammed along the middle, and the gun tucked right in between, nestled gingerly among the most padded clothes so that it wasn't knocking against the hard material of the luggage case. The last thing Benedikt Montagov needed was an accidental misfiring when he hauled his luggage onto the train, so he had packed very carefully. He knew this, and yet, as he stood there in the line outside Yaroslavsky Station, he was suddenly doubtful.

"I have to check again," Benedikt said.

Marshall Seo was holding his own luggage out in an instant, providing a flat surface to prevent Benedikt from jostling the line when he lifted his bag. The temperature was freezing, snow clumped in mounds along the sides of the pavement. With a grateful expression, Benedikt hefted his luggage case to rest on Marshall's and undid the latches with his gloved fingers, running a careful eye over the contents. This was the sixth time he had checked since they'd left their apartment, and though Benedikt had most definitely packed everything he needed for their weeklong journey on the Trans-Siberian Express, there was still an unrelenting urge to keep looking, as if something might change despite the laws of physics and cause their plans to go horrifically awry.

Marshall's face popped into his view suddenly, obscuring the luggage contents before Benedikt finished his examination. Marshall had craned his whole body sideways so that he could look up at Benedikt, nearly resembling a corkscrew despite the anatomical limitations of the human spine.

"Everything is well?" Marshall asked.

Benedikt reached his hand out, smooshing the entire palm of his cold glove into his husband's face before pushing him away. "Yes. Yes, I think so. Now don't do that—you're going to pull a back muscle."

Marshall righted himself with a grin, rolling out his shoulders as Benedikt closed his luggage case begrudgingly, both of them shuffling forward. At his full height, Marshall was at least two heads taller than the group of elderly women gossiping in front of them, but once he finished stretching to ensure he hadn't pulled anything, he returned to his slouch, and he was again at perfect eye level with Benedikt. They were only a few feet away from the entrance into Yaroslavsky Station, and there weren't many people in front of them anyhow, but the thick winter coats taking up space in the line made the wait seem endless.

"Don't even remind me about my traitorous back," Marshall said. "Twenty-three years old and I could get a cramp from breathing wrong."

Benedikt blinked. He did the math in his head. "Mars, you're twenty-four."

Without warning, Marshall dropped to his knees, trembling with the drama. "I'm *aging*!"

The old ladies turned around with some concern. Benedikt hurried to haul Marshall back up, widening his eyes in warning but unable to fully commit to the chastising. Marshall was only trying to distract him. He knew Marshall better than he knew himself sometimes, and when Marshall Seo got overly theatrical, it was usually because he wanted Benedikt to stop frantically spinning in his own head and pay attention to him instead.

"You're trying to get us told off for being a public nuisance," Benedikt muttered.

"I could switch gears if you want to get told off for public obscenity instead," Marshall replied. He puckered for a kiss.

"*Marshall.*"

"Love you too. Line's moving."

Benedikt forced himself to look stern. Marshall was hardly bothered, wearing a wide grin when they finally entered Yaroslavsky Station. Inside, a ticket attendant was checking passengers as they passed through the line, so slowly that one would think the Trans-Siberian Express wasn't running on a tight schedule. Whether at the start of the route or along any of the multiple stops on the way to Vladivostok, the train would start running when it was supposed to run, and passengers either watched the time carefully or got left behind.

"Ben," Marshall said, turning slightly more somber as he reached into his coat for their two tickets. "It'll be all right, you know."

He didn't clarify what he was talking about, but he didn't have to.

"Who said anything to the contrary?" Benedikt retorted.

Marshall looked askance at him, one eyebrow lifting smoothly. When he turned his head, the gloomy morning light glowed around his pitch-black hair, thick and smooth and eternally untangled no matter how many times Benedikt ran his fingers through it. He had an urge to do it now, but Marshall was easily spurred into mischief, and then they really would get marked for public obscenity.

"Your frequency with this"—Marshall tapped on Benedikt's luggage case, indicating the amount of times he had opened and closed it—"increases the more you fret about something else. Everything will go smoothly. Think happy thoughts. Food carts. Snow-capped mountains. My dazzling smile."

Benedikt punched Marshall lightly on the shoulder. Still . . . his words did help. They always did.

At the front of the line, Marshall passed their tickets forward, flashing that smile of his. The attendant ripped a notch into the tickets without looking for longer than a second. Gave the slips back. Waved them through.

"Platform number one," Benedikt reminded.

"You're my only number one," Marshall replied, somewhat nonsensically.

A flurry of freezing wind blew around them. The train loomed up ahead, the steam funnels on the head carriage rising into the smoggy air, its engine already rumbling. The chains around its sides rattled with every gust, like an orchestral welcome while the passengers boarded. Their tickets put them in soft-class, among the first few carriages with either one or two beds to every compartment, which fortunately meant they wouldn't be sharing a room with strangers.

"I beg of you," Benedikt said, starting his climb up the steps, careful to hold the handrail so he wouldn't slip on the ice-cold metal. "Stop flirting with me while we're on an important mission."

Though Benedikt didn't swivel around to look, he knew that Marshall had a sly expression while he proceeded after him. "Can't I? You don't look like a married man. Seems like delicious low-hanging fruit to me."

They had left their wedding rings at home—there was no use playing with fire while traveling. As perpetually ready as Marshall was to finish a fight against anyone trying to start one, they really were on a tight schedule for this trip and had no time to be getting into arguments with bigots. If anyone asked, they were room-mates.

"Don't you dare bite me when I least expect it."

Marshall only clacked his teeth in response. With the slightest twitch of his lips, Benedikt entered the carriage and shook his hair out, getting rid of the water droplets that had condensed in his blond curls from the cold. A gray-haired woman strode toward him immediately: the provodnitsa, coming to check tickets. She hesitated for a second when making eye contact with Marshall, but he extended their tickets and asked about her day in Russian, establishing himself as a native instead of a foreigner before a snap judgment could be made.

Marshall was far better at mimicking the Moscow accent than Benedikt was. They both had rather irregular ways of speaking when they weren't watching themselves, the result of learning the language from Russians in Shanghai who had come from all over the place, fleeing war or oppressive regimes. Where Benedikt had a hard time telling the difference between which parts of his speech were mere habits and which were proper rules, Marshall had long learned how to adjust in public. It didn't matter as much for Benedikt. Hiding in the Soviet Union had been a matter of safety while the Nationalists were after them in Shanghai, but here, his face gave him the privilege of blending in and brushing away questions before they were even asked.

"All the way to Vladivostok?" the provodnitsa said, eyeing the print on their tickets.

A clatter of footfalls sounded from the steps outside, bringing in more passengers who were embarking. From the corner of Benedikt's eye, he caught sight of a man squeezing into the carriage despite the orderly procession, pushing close to the provodnitsa and offering his ticket even while she was already holding two.

The provodnitsa eyed him, unimpressed. He was Russian, a briefcase clutched tight in his other hand. Benedikt would have marked him to be in his fifties, but when he discounted the deep-carved forehead wrinkles, he wondered if the man was younger in actuality and only prematurely haggard.

"Sir, please hold on."

"Just take it, would you? I have business to attend to."

Before the provodnitsa could clutch the ticket properly, he had shoved it against her shoulder and pushed through the passageway, striding fast into his allocated compartment and slamming the door closed.

"Chert poberi," Marshall muttered. "Someone woke up on the wrong side of the bed."

But the old provodnitsa looked unfazed, likely used to rude passengers. She folded their two tickets, pursing her lips. Though the Trans-Siberian Express's last stop was Vladivostok, many had destinations along the way instead, needing to be ushered off by the provodnitsa in those few minutes that the train paused at that station. She had a lot to keep track of.

"Lucky for you two, you're right next door to him. Go on and get settled."

Marshall was prodding for Benedikt to hurry along before Benedikt had registered the instruction. They maneuvered out of the way, shuffling into the compartment and dropping their luggage on the floor. The room was small despite the luxury of a soft-class ticket, which was far more expensive than hard-class carriages near the back of the train. The two categorizations were named plainly to represent their arrangements: where the more expensive ticket in soft-class got additional space and nicer decorations, hard-class was crammed with four to a room.

"A bunk bed," Marshall remarked as he closed the door after them, taking inventory of their room. "Are you going to miss the warmth of my embrace at night?"

"I'm actually going to have such a great time freed from the relentless twitching you do in your sleep."

Marshall was quick to protest the accusation, making a scowl. The two of them alone at last, Benedikt finally felt some of the weight lift off his shoulders, his tense mood fading away. They were on board. The train would release its whine of steam and begin to move when the clock struck the minute of departure, and nothing was going to go wrong.

Benedikt reached out, a hand sliding along the back of Marshall's neck, then up, up, into his thick crop of hair. When his fingers threaded in, Benedikt felt all his remaining tension bleed away from his spine, slithering to the floor like a shed skin.

"I'm joking, Mars. If you decide to sleep on the separate bunk, I'm going to assume our relationship is under strain."

In a flash, Marshall's scowl turned into a grin. "Relax, *I'm* only pretending. Don't forget"—there was a glint in his eye when he tapped a finger to the inside of Benedikt's wrist, right at the point where his pulse was beating—"you were the one who admitted you were in love with me first. You can't fool me."

Benedikt rolled his eyes, removing his hand with a huff, but his chest warmed a few degrees nevertheless.

Sometimes Benedikt didn't know how to handle the extent of the feelings living in his heart. Almost five years had passed with his love in the open instead of trapped in the dark, and it would still blink its bewildered eyes when it was seen clearly, surprised to have been acknowledged. He had assumed that there wouldn't be much change: he had grown up with Marshall Seo, after all; he had already been sharing an apartment and most of his life with him before Marshall went and faked his death and drove Benedikt to such depths of anguish that everything he had pushed down and down and down came surging to the surface.

But there was a stark difference between Marshall's patient, controlled love, burning on low while he waited for Benedikt to shake himself into order, and Marshall's unabashed love, given the kindling to blaze. It was the whisper of contact when he grabbed Marshall's shoulder to say goodbye leaving their apartment in Shanghai, contrasted with the whole-body hug that Marshall gave him at the doorway of their smaller one-bedroom in Moscow, laughing when Benedikt said he absolutely had to go and laughing harder when Benedikt didn't actually attempt to extricate himself. It was a longing glance across the kitchen in the days before, measured against reaching over the counter without hesitation now—thumbs brushing along cheekbones, legs flung over laps, lips colliding and colliding with the softest impact.

He had never even considered what he was missing until he had it. He couldn't imagine the same thrill replicated with anyone other than Marshall.

When he thought about it too much, though, everything existing inside him felt so big that he was sure his veins had outgrown their circulatory system and were seconds away from pushing out of his skin. At present, he couldn't deal with any of the onslaught except by giving Marshall a great, big shove, exhibiting his emotions with a physical *whack!*

"Ow," Marshall complained, even though it didn't hurt. He shuffled a few steps before regaining his balance. "Please treat your lover with more tender care."

Benedikt unlatched his luggage case—this time, at least, it was to unpack rather than to check the contents for the umpteenth time.

"I thought you were my roommate."

"We can't be roommates who kiss?"

Benedikt threw a rolled-up pair of socks at his husband. "*Unpack,* Mars."

With a laugh, Marshall hauled his luggage case onto one of the side tables and started to shake his clothes free. The two of them usually lived quite simply, given that their only source of income came from teaching art classes to little kids in the neighborhood. Benedikt did the actual teaching; Marshall did the bookkeeping and the advertising, plastering posters on every streetlamp. Surprisingly, they did get enough parents flowing in and out to subsist off the earnings.

These train tickets hadn't come from those earnings, though. They had come from Benedikt's cousin, Roma, who was running an illegal weapons ring with his wife in a small township a few hours outside of Shanghai—a business in which he and Juliette most certainly made ten times more than what Benedikt and Marshall did. Typical of two former gang heirs to walk away from that life and then somehow wander back into it anyway, just without the intergenerational blood feud.

"I cannot emphasize the severity of this situation enough," Roma had said after giving his instructions, his voice tight over the phone. "Someone's life depends on it. I need your help to get Lourens into Zhouzhuang as soon as possible."

"Who's *someone*?" Benedikt had asked out of curiosity, holding the receiver tight against his ear and furrowing his brow, glancing at Marshall across the room. Marshall hadn't been paying attention at first when Benedikt picked up the call, but he'd looked up fast as soon as he realized it was Roma on the other end of the line. Roma or Juliette usually had set times that they called so that they wouldn't be missed—and Marshall and Juliette certainly hated missing their gossiping sessions—so the telephone ringing with an unscheduled call from Zhouzhuang was unexpected.

"Have you been reading Shanghai's newspapers recently?"

Benedikt scrunched his nose. He tried to avoid bringing newspapers into the house if they were reporting on international news: the last thing Marshall needed was to see his father's face without warning.

"I'm a bit tuned out."

"Let's just say that Juliette's side of the family is in a bit of trouble. Actually, scratch that—they're in a lot of trouble . . . international war–level trouble."

Benedikt shook himself out of his reverie, unfolding his shirt and hanging it in the little nook beside the bunk bed.

"When we get to Vladivostok, we have to find Lourens within hours to make the train into Harbin," he said to Marshall, if only to hear their plan aloud once more. "Or else we won't make the earliest train into Tianjin. And then we'll miss the next train into Suzhou."

And from Suzhou, they would have to drive an hour by car before finally arriving in Zhouzhuang. The route wouldn't have needed such an intensive plan if they took the last train leg into a major city with plenty of rail activity, like Nanjing or Shanghai, but Nanjing was a key capital crawling with Nationalists, and Shanghai was even more dangerous for getting spotted and hauled in. They could hardly bring Lourens for help if the three of them were marked en route as former White Flowers and taken in for execution.

All to say: Benedikt was stressed. It wasn't only the train schedule that they were up against, either. Vladivostok to Harbin ran on what was once the Chinese Eastern Railway, a shortcut that diverged from the Trans-Siberian line and passed through Manchuria instead of around. But Manchuria was under the control of the Japanese now, and in journeying through that territory, Benedikt and Marshall could only hope that they weren't stopped by a soldier making trouble with their entry papers or some larger conflict on the land that pulled all passenger transport to a halt. Each step of this journey had to go smoothly if they were to get to their final destination in time.

Once they left Vladivostok, it would be another two days of traveling, give or take. They would have to squeeze in their sleep during the train rides, which was a risk when the stops didn't come with station announcements and they needed to pay attention to when they were getting off. For now, at least, Benedikt and Marshall had these seven days until they had to fret about what was coming next.

"I am most concerned about whether we can get Lourens to come along once we find him," Marshall said. "Do we have a plan if he refuses?"

"We kidnap him," Benedikt replied easily.

"Are you going to pistol-whip him into shape?"

Benedikt shot over a brief glance. He put his gun on the shelf. "Would you like me to?"

"Now who's the one flirting?"

Before Benedikt could throw his hands up in defeat, the floor jolted beneath him. The tracks emitted a loud screech, and the train's heavy wheels began to turn. Each clank of metal and clatter of chains strained through the glass of the compartment window with effort. Then the whole train shook once, and they were moving, pulling away from Yaroslavsky Station with little other warning.

Marshall went to stand by the window, staring out at the snowy white landscape, his hands shoved into his pockets.

"Honestly," he started, "this might even be fun."

Coming from anyone else's mouth, Benedikt might have fumed at the very idea that such a stressful assignment with someone else's life at stake could possibly be *fun*. But it was Marshall, and Marshall brought genuine levity anywhere he went no matter how dark the night grew, so Benedikt only walked over too, joining him by the window as the train picked up speed.

"Whatever you say," Benedikt replied, knocking their shoulders together. "All aboard the Trans-Siberian Express."

2

Marshall was eavesdropping on the grouchy man next door.

He hadn't intended to. He had only wandered out into the passageway to find the provodnitsa, hoping to have some tea, but she was nowhere to be seen, so he had ambled down to the samovar himself for boiling water.

Then he heard the muffled argument.

"*. . . you can't . . . ridiculous!*"

Marshall paused, hands wrapped around his thermos. There was clearly someone else in the compartment with the man, but their voice was too quiet to be heard, and the train itself was always humming with the noise of its journey. On occasion, the whole carriage felt like it was bouncing on its tracks, hitting certain sections of the rail that were built in a peculiar way.

"They've been arguing for quite some time."

Marshall's grip tightened on his thermos, startled by the voice behind him, but he managed not to jump before he turned around. A short, middle-aged man had poked his head out from the compartment on the left. If Marshall could hear the occasional snippets from his compartment on the right, surely the same would be wafting in the other direction.

"Do you know who he is?" Marshall asked.

The man paused, then nodded. "Danila Andreyevich Popov.

He introduced himself when we almost collided on the way to the toilet. Seemed to be in a terrible rush."

What rush could there possibly be aboard a moving train? It had been late afternoon when they set off. Now that they were a few hours into their journey, night was rapidly falling, directing passengers toward the dining carriage as stomachs started to growl and body clocks started to adjust to their own schedules. From Moscow to Vladivostok they would be passing eight different time zones. Soon it would become impossible to follow one watch.

"And the other party?"

The man shook his head. Where Marshall thought the stranger had been making an expression of surprise earlier while remarking on the ongoing argument, he was now realizing that the man had permanently large eyes, pulled wide and expressive no matter the topic.

"I had a peek earlier when the door was open: this is a solo compartment. Only a visitor, not a roommate." At that, there was a grumble from within his room, a voice asking him to keep it down, and the man peered inside, nose wrinkling. "Wish I could afford a solo compartment too. I am Stepan Maximovich Ivanov. You are?"

"Just Marshall," Marshall replied nicely. Ever since their move to Moscow, it had been amusing for him to make up different patronymics each time he met someone new, since he hardly cared to adopt his real father's name into his own by Russian custom. But this train ride was going to be seven days long, and he didn't want to lose track of the names he was giving to his fellow passengers, nor did he have the commitment to pick a favorite false one. Besides, when they exchanged vows, Benedikt had refused to let him change his Korean last name, saying that he was going to take it too and he wouldn't accept anything else. If Marshall came up with a proper Russian alias, he would make Benedikt upset.

"A pleasure to make your acquaintance," the man—Stepan—said. "Do excuse me now, I must shut up for my traveling companion." He slid his compartment door closed, and Marshall proceeded back into his own room, inhaling the steam that was drifting from his thermos full of boiling water.

When Marshall returned, Benedikt was sitting on the lower bunk, bent over his sketchbook. He had a smudge of pencil on his chin, smeared in a half circle, as if he had pressed a finger there in thought without realizing there was graphite all over his hand. It made a typical sight: whenever Benedikt lost himself in his art, the world would cease to exist around him. Marshall might be able to get an answer out of him if he was asking what he wanted for dinner, but as much as Marshall loved chatter, he never wanted to keep pushing for conversation if Benedikt was concentrating hard. Marshall preferred watching him instead—watching his mouth purse in thought as he measured dimensions, watching small wrinkles appear at the side of his eyes while he narrowed his gaze to study what he had already put down.

The only time that Marshall had interrupted Benedikt without remorse had been two years ago, for his quiet, unplanned, *"Will you marry me?"* They had been sitting in the living room, tending to separate tasks. Early evening, the purple sunset outside bleeding its shadows along the carpet. A warming April, the window left open a crack to offset the district heating.

"What?" Benedikt had asked suddenly, seeming to doubt whether he had heard correctly.

"I know there's no one here to attend a wedding," Marshall went on, "and it would be a bad idea to get legal papers in the event that we are endangered. Nonetheless, even if we officiate it ourselves in a garden somewhere, I wanted to ask. Will you marry me?"

Benedikt had stared at him for what felt like eons. He remained unspeaking for long enough that Marshall twitched, a layer of sweat prickling at his neck. The pipes in the house started to splutter, and Marshall, too, added, "It's okay if you don't want—"

Then Benedikt lunged over, shaking him by the shoulders to interrupt. "Yes. Of course. Of course it's a yes. You just took me by surprise." He paused, touching a finger to Marshall's forehead and looking delighted to find a sheen of cold sweat. "Mars."

Marshall swatted at his hand. "Stop that. I'm just warm."

"Now you know how I felt the first time I said I loved you."

"Oh, absolutely not. You *yelled* at me, Ben."

"Fondly!"

Marshall couldn't resist laughing then. He couldn't resist wrapping his arms around Benedikt as tightly as he could, because it was unimaginable that they had ended up here, unimaginable that they had been removed from so much, yet the thing he'd wanted most had been granted. Through their youth, he would have been glad to have Benedikt by his side forever and ever as his best friend; he would have been content to keep his feelings to himself if Benedikt had never returned them, gratified just to ache from a distance. But he didn't have to. *He didn't have to.*

"I needed to be the one to ask," he had murmured into Benedikt's neck, still clutching onto their embrace. "Who knows whether you might have waited another ten years like the first time."

Benedikt looked up now in the train compartment, his lashes blinking golden even in the terrible lighting.

"What?" he asked suddenly, a perfect echo to Marshall's memory.

Marshall set down the thermos and walked closer, coming to a stop beside Benedikt and propping one arm on the wooden structure of the top bunk. The beds were made with the lower bunk jutting a bit farther out, so that Benedikt wouldn't hit his head while he sat there, his face tilted up to look at Marshall looming over him.

With a careful hand, Marshall brushed away the graphite smear.

"You have something here."

"Do I?" Benedikt asked. His chin was clean again. "Did you get it?"

"No," Marshall lied, already leaning down. "Don't move, I'll try again."

When he kissed him, it was like breathing a deep gulp of summer air, like the first fall of snow landing crisp and cold on his skin. Marshall Seo was fundamentally a temperamental person: a fast driver, a reckless fighter, prone to taking leaps off of three-story buildings instead of finding the stairs. But Benedikt grounded him. Benedikt Montagov moved through the world with such intricate care—his steps calculated, his thought process tunneling miles deep—that Marshall would stick around for ten lifetimes trying to figure him out.

He never would figure him out, of course, which was the fun of it.

A tug came on his shirt collar. Though Marshall's arm was still gripping the bunk for balance, he complied easily with the motion, letting Benedikt pull him closer.

"I don't know if you noticed," Benedikt started when they parted for breath, "but the walls are quite thin."

"I'm very aware," Marshall replied. As if on cue, there was a loud thump on the adjoining wall, and he frowned, turning to look instead of leaning in again. Reluctantly, the two of them stilled, listening for further noise, wondering whether it had been a warning knock because they'd been too loud.

Then there was another thump . . . not against the wall, but the sound of something heavy hitting the floorboards instead.

Silence.

"What was that?" Benedikt asked. His voice had dropped to a whisper.

"I don't know," Marshall whispered back. He wasn't sure why they were even taking care to be quiet. They waited a while longer, trying to envision what could possibly be going on in Danila Andreyevich's room to cause such a ruckus, but there was nothing more.

Only a gurgle from their own room, which could be attributed to Marshall's stomach.

Benedikt glanced at his wristwatch for the time, then poked Marshall's chest. "Let's go to the dining car."

"Must we?" Marshall tried to catch Benedikt's hand. Benedikt only poked him again, more aggressively.

"Come on, solnishko."

They composed themselves and entered the passageway. Marshall very narrowly avoided colliding with a girl who was hurrying by with her thermos, pressing against the wall to let her pass. She glanced up briefly, flashing a polite smile before proceeding into the next carriage. Marshall and Benedikt went in the other direction, walking only a few steps before sliding open the door to the dining car, one carriage over. The strong aroma of something tomato-like hit Marshall's nose immediately, though there seemed to be a variety of dishes laid out in front of the passengers who had already found seats and started to dine. White tablecloths adorned each setup, topped with a glass vase holding a single daisy. The train bounced, jostling utensils against plates and passengers standing shoulder to shoulder around the bar at the back.

"Gentlemen!"

Marshall ignored the voice at first, still inspecting the tables and looking for free seats. When the voice came again, however, Benedikt nudged his elbow and whispered, "I think he's talking to us."

At one of the tables, there was a boy sitting alone, waving eagerly. He was just a kid—fifteen years old, maybe younger. His muddy brown hair stuck up in two different directions, as though he had been intent on brushing everything smooth before a strong gust of wind had its own ideas about what was currently in style.

He was also dressed in a Western suit one size too big, the shoulders stiff and square upon his small frame.

"Hello," Marshall returned. "Do we know you?"

The boy shot up to his feet, seeing that he had succeeded in inciting conversation. Abandoning the bowl of soup at his table, he hurried in front of Benedikt and Marshall, extending his hand.

"Lev Grigoryevich Vodin. How do you do?"

Hesitantly, Marshall shook Lev's hand. "Where are your parents?"

"My uncle is the train officer on board, actually," Lev replied. "And I am an aspiring journalist. Do you have time for some questions?"

Benedikt nudged Marshall's elbow again. It was a signal that said, *Absolutely not.* Benedikt was usually great with children, especially toddlers, but Lev Grigoryevich seemed just old enough to press into the busybody almost-adult category instead. The boy was bobbing up and down on his toes so eagerly, though, and Marshall thought it would be too mean to turn him down.

"I feel rather famished at the moment, so perhaps later," he replied. "You can find me at—"

A terrifying scream pierced through the train.

Benedikt swiveled around so fast that Marshall felt the air turn frigid around him. A second scream tore into their surroundings again—from the same source, high-pitched and feminine. The moment Marshall turned and lunged in that direction, unthinking, Benedikt snagged his elbow, hissing, "Wait, wait."

"Ben, someone might need help—"

"Well, does it *have* to be you—"

"Ben!"

"All right, all right—"

Then Benedikt surged forward, back the way they had come, pushing past the door and returning to the soft-class carriage.

"Hey!" Marshall called after him. He remained still for a moment, thrown off by the switch in roles, before hurrying through the door too. Why was Benedikt like this? "I didn't mean you should go *without* me—"

As soon as his shoes skidded against the carpet of the carriage, Marshall almost slammed right into his husband. He reached out quickly, grabbing Benedikt's shoulders to steady himself. Before he could ask why Benedikt had stopped, he saw the provodnitsa outside Danila Andreyevich Popov's room. She was heaving to fill her lungs. It didn't take much to conclude that she had been the one screaming, since her face was as pale as a sheet of ice. Marshall wanted to believe that she had simply seen something unsavory—perhaps the room was too messy, perhaps there was a rodent that had chewed its way into the compartments. But the knees of her trousers were covered in blood, as was one of her hands, coated up to the wrist.

"He's dead!" she cried. "There's a murderer on board!"

3

Without missing a beat, Benedikt lunged past the provodnitsa and barged into the room. He hardly considered that he wasn't supposed to be present at the scene, nor did he care much if in a minute or so there would be someone coming around to yell at him. The provodnitsa had seen him approach. It was evident that he had newly shown up and had nothing to do with the crime. There was no problem, surely, with him taking a look.

"Oh dear."

Marshall had followed him in, his voice sounding over Benedikt's shoulder. The man was prone on the floor. It was rather hard to tell that he was surrounded by blood because of the dark carpet, which explained why the provodnitsa's knees had been bloodied. She must have knelt to check on him before realizing what had happened.

The puddle, Benedikt realized upon scanning the carpet closely, was rather large too. Where was the wound? A gunshot to the chest? A blow to the head?

He crept forward a fraction. Although the dead body was face-down with its stomach pressed to the floor, the head was tilted ever so slightly toward the window at the other side of the room. As if something was preventing it from following the direction of the rest of the body.

Benedikt hovered over the dead man, trying to see onto his far side. He caught sight of an object lodged in his throat. *Ah.* That explained the amount of blood.

"What *is* that?" Marshall asked.

"It looks like a fountain pen," Benedikt answered. He signaled for the provodnitsa, who was trembling in the passageway. "Did you find him like this?"

The provodnitsa nodded. She swallowed hard, having gotten all the screaming out of her system. "I . . . I wanted to check up on him." With the back of her arm, to avoid dirtying her face with the blood on her hands, she pushed a strand of disheveled gray hair out of her eyes. "I knocked briefly a few minutes ago, but there was no answer. When I finished making my rounds in the rest of the carriage, I simply let myself in. It is customary, in case the passenger is too busy to open their door."

"*Make way! Make way!*"

There was a sudden whistle in the passageway, then a uniformed man bustling into the compartment and scrunching his nose at the sight. Other curious passengers had shuffled close, and the train officer gestured quickly for everyone to vacate. He could barely be heard past all the horrified whispers; suddenly half the train's soft-class passengers were clustered in the passageway to gawk at the body, rising onto the tips of their toes and getting close to the provodnitsa.

"Please step out and make some space!" the officer bellowed. He waved vigorously at the two attendants hovering in the passageway at the back of the crowd. "Someone get Mrs. Kuzmina a towel so she doesn't have to stand here covered with blood."

The attendants hurried to the front of the crowd. As Benedikt followed Marshall out of the compartment, shooed from the scene, he kept his attention on what was unfolding. While the other passengers started to shift away, grimacing at the thought of watching the body get carried out past them, he grabbed Marshall's elbow and prompted him to hold still, listening to the rest of the conversation.

"What can we do, Mr. Vodin?" one of the attendants said nervously. "Shouldn't . . . shouldn't we leave it in place until the police can come?"

Vodin, the officer, had propped his hands on his hips. He was a large, burly man, with a thick mustache curling at his upper lip.

"Hmm," he said. "I suppose you are correct. Leave the body in place. Clear the crowd outside and escort these onlookers away. We will halt the train at the next stop."

"They can't," Marshall hissed suddenly, his words meant only for Benedikt. "A delay like that will throw us off schedule."

"Yes, but someone just got murdered," Benedikt replied. He grimaced. "What are they going to do, *not* summon the police?"

"Ben." Marshall's grip tightened on his elbow. "Roma was very clear. We have someone's *life* depending on us."

"But what can *we* do? *Become* the police?"

Marshall's expression brightened. As soon as he released Benedikt's elbow and hurried back into the room, Benedikt cursed under his breath, because he knew Marshall had probably just gotten a terrible idea.

"Officer!" he crowed. "There's no need to summon the police. We are private investigators, and we can take on this case."

By God. This was even worse than terrible. This was the worst idea known to mankind.

"That is convenient and all," Vodin was saying when Benedikt pushed past the onlookers to join Marshall, "but we will still need the police—"

"The door between the soft-class carriages and the hard-class carriages was locked for departure, correct?" Marshall cut in. "Keep it locked, post a guard there to prevent any movement between the carriage classes. We are aboard a moving train, officer. As long as no one gets on and no one gets off, that means the culprit responsible for this murder remains within one of these four soft-class carriages. And you know it is absolutely not us, because we were talking to your nephew in the dining carriage."

The passengers who were still hovering nearby had turned quiet. Some looked pale. The provodnitsa—Mrs. Kuzmina—remained too, having shifted from terrified to dazed.

Vodin, on the other hand, rubbed his chin thoughtfully. "You know my nephew, do you?"

A squeak sounded through the crowd. Benedikt cast a glance over and spotted Lev trying to push through.

"Since he was away at the time of this crime as well," Marshall continued, gesturing at the body on the floor, "he might be a great help as a journalist. Think about your alternative: When you stop for the police, what will happen?" He put his hands behind his back and did a slow circle on his heel, as if he was really musing on the situation. Benedikt felt like he was watching a whole production at work. "The doors open, passengers get off, and a killer flees into the world forever. Mr. Popov seemed like an important man. Won't you be the one punished for that when every lead dries up? I imagine you have people to report to—people who will want answers for a death that occurred on board."

The captivated audience mumbled and murmured, shifting on their feet in concern. The attendant at the doorway tried to dismiss the passengers from the scene to no avail. If anything, there was further movement, plenty of jostling and complaining, before Lev finally burst through the gaps, charging into the room.

"Uncle, uncle," Lev Grigoryevich exclaimed, holding a camera in his hands. "You should allow them to investigate."

"Lev," the officer chided. "Everybody out. Immediately. Clear this passageway."

The attendants made a greater effort now at dismissal, and the passengers were shooed off in both directions, some returning to their rooms and others to their abandoned dinners in the dining car. The attendant who had been concerned about not touching the body took Mrs. Kuzmina by the elbow, helping her toward the washroom to rinse off. Eventually it was only Benedikt and Marshall in the passageway, with Marshall casting Benedikt an assured smile and Benedikt scrunching his nose. Lev and his uncle were whispering in front of the closed compartment, not loud enough to pick out what they were saying, but by tone alone, it seemed the boy really wanted the investigation. He gestured to his camera. Waved it around and mimicked taking pictures.

Eventually, Vodin patted his nephew's shoulder, seeming to come to an agreement about something. He stepped around Lev and approached Benedikt and Marshall with his hand extended.

"Your names, gentlemen?"

"Just Marshall." Marshall brought his hand out to shake. He tightened his grip to the point that even Benedikt spotted the indents of his knuckles flashing white. "A pleasure to be of service."

"And you?" Vodin asked, turning to Benedikt.

"Benedikt Ivanovich." He didn't offer to shake.

Vodin looked from him to Marshall, withdrawing his hand. "Is this an order of the profession? Surely you both have family names."

Marshall's expression flashed into panic for a brief moment. Before he decided to come up with a lie, Benedikt took the attention smoothly, answering: "Sokov. I am Benedikt Ivanovich Sokov. Perfectly normal, no?"

"Thank you, Mr. Sokov." Vodin inclined his head. He turned over his shoulder again, and when Lev grinned from where he remained, the officer sighed deeply. "While half of our travelers are heading directly for Vladivostok, you must understand that many other passengers bought tickets with destinations along the route.

They will not be pleased with this turn in events. We are essentially holding them hostage."

"But you cannot risk the killer departing," Benedikt said firmly, finally playing along with Marshall's plan. It looked like it might actually be working. "This is the best way to ensure justice. Have the train proceed nonstop to its final destination. We will have a culprit for you by our arrival in Vladivostok."

For a long moment, Vodin regarded them, his mustache taking up half his face and his stare overwhelming the other half.

"My nephew has convinced me that this is the best course of action, so I have decided to trust him," he finally said. "However, I would like an update in twenty-four hours. Depending on your progress, I will decide then whether it is a good idea to continue nonstop or halt the train and call in the police."

"Maybe we will even have the culprit found in twenty-four hours!" Marshall declared.

Vodin didn't look convinced. He looked over his shoulder again, nodding to Lev, and while his gaze was turned away, Benedikt smacked Marshall in a quick motion, his arm colliding with a hard stomach. *Tone it down,* he was saying.

"While you investigate," Vodin continued, "Lev will accompany you and take some remarks. He will report back to me to save you the time, but you may find me directly if there is anything you need. Can I leave you to survey the crime scene?"

Marshall nodded.

With a shake of his head, as if he couldn't believe he was allowing this, Vodin went to open the door, speaking to Lev again.

"Did you . . . use my name?" Marshall, meanwhile, leaned over to whisper to Benedikt.

"You do not like it?"

Marshall grinned. "I like it very much, Mr. Sokov."

The compartment opened again. Vodin took his leave without

further dillydallying, clapping his nephew's arm in farewell before using that same hand to carefully push through into the next carriage.

"All right," Benedikt said, rolling his sleeves up. "How hard can this be? Watch where you are stepping."

"Are you talking to me or the kid?" Marshall asked, following Benedikt in.

"The kid. Unless you are some amateur. Find a good place to stand, Lev Grigoryevich."

There was no response to his instruction. Concerned, Benedikt turned back to locate the kid and found that he had gone pale, staring intently at the body. Lev hovered there for a considerable moment before his hand flew to his mouth. At once, he ran out of the room in the direction of the washroom.

Benedikt sighed. *How hard can this be?* He really shouldn't have asked.

4

Night had fallen thoroughly, offering only velvet darkness on the other side of the window. Every so often, a railside light would flash into the room, but otherwise the overhead bulb was their only illumination, and it wasn't great as far as lighting sources went.

Marshall eyed the body. He didn't want to move the corpse in case it messed up some clue, but in truth, he also didn't want to go touching any stiff limbs, even with gloves on. While the kid stood at a distance, scribbling in his notebook and probably writing down every word that Marshall and Benedikt said to each other, Benedikt was digging around the room itself, searching through the deceased's belongings.

"His name was Danila Andreyevich Popov," Marshall reported while he carefully prodded a finger at Popov's clothes, checking if there was anything that might shake out. "He introduced himself to the man next door, Stepan. And I had a conversation with Stepan about the arguing we both heard coming from his room. Probably no less than ten minutes before he was killed."

"Then I suppose the person you heard arguing with him was the killer," Benedikt stated plainly. He was fiddling with something in the corner of the room.

"I am inclined to agree." Marshall rose to his feet, rolling out the strain in his neck. "The unfortunate part is that I couldn't discern anything about the voice. It was too faint. They were trying their best to keep quiet."

"Hmmm . . ."

Benedikt continued to investigate, deep in thought. Marshall, too, circled around the man again, trying to look at the body from the head instead of from the toes. He didn't want to get too close and step in the blood. It was starting to smell—like rusting iron and something rancid. By tomorrow, the scene would turn rather unpleasant. They would have to do a final examination in the daytime and then simply suffer the consequences of moving the body. It wasn't as if taking pictures would help if there was no darkroom on the train to develop them. By the time they developed the pictures off-board, the case would be irrelevant to their interests. They were only playing detective to prevent the train from stopping.

"Mr. Marshall, do you have any observations?" Lev called from the compartment entrance. After heaving up his stomach in the washroom, he had eagerly scuttled back into the room and snapped a few pictures. Before he could get light-headed again from the scene, Marshall had maneuvered him firmly away from the body, pressing the kid up against the closed door. If it were up to him, he would have put Lev on the other side instead, but chances were high that Vodin was only allowing this investigation to happen because his nephew wanted some journalism practice out of it.

"I hope you know that most journalists are not asking investigators for their observations *at* the crime scene," Marshall returned. He grimaced. "Ink nib, stabbed straight through his throat. There's the faintest protrusion at the back of his neck, but the metal didn't break the skin there. A bit more pressure would have done the trick."

He didn't add that it looked like there had to have been considerable struggle before the man died. His mouth was open a fraction, frozen in his struggled gasp for breath. The pen wasn't thick enough to completely block out his windpipe, so he would have been viciously heaving and choking in his last moments before he bled out.

"Don't forget about the coat stand," Benedikt supplied. He had moved on to examining the bed, shaking through the blankets.

Of the four walls in the compartment, one hosted the door, one hosted the window, one held the bed, and the fourth bore nothing save for a few old scuff marks. At its base, however, the coat stand had been broken in two, snapped right down the middle, and the two pieces left on the carpet.

"Right," Marshall said. "There's a scratch on Mr. Popov's forehead. My best guess . . ."

He pointed to one of the sharp hooks on the coat stand. They were made of metal.

"Either he was struck and then stabbed or stabbed and then struck."

Lev grimaced. Though he was turning pale again, he jotted down the observations faithfully.

"I am not seeing anything else around the room." Benedikt took a step back from the messy sheets. There was nothing more to rummage around. These compartments were already miniature to begin with. "Lev, ask your uncle for all the information stored about this man. Anything that can be helpful."

In an instant, the boy saluted, then snapped his notebook closed and hurried out of the compartment. Marshall scuffed his foot against one half of the coat stand, turning over the circular object to see if there was anything interesting on the other side. There was not.

"This feels very nostalgic," he said. "We used to look at so many dead bodies together."

"And I suppose that alone qualifies us as private investigators," Benedikt replied dryly.

"Why not? The first thing any job needs is work experience."

Benedikt rolled his eyes, but a hint of humor quirked at his lips. As much as Benedikt made it his job to keep Marshall in line, Marshall always knew exactly what it took to get through.

"I did find something, actually. Is the door closed?"

The floor bounced under their feet. They had been driving for long enough to hit the rougher parts of the tracks, out in places that never saw travelers except for the screech of a train passing in the night.

Marshall glanced to the door. "Closed firm."

Benedikt was holding something in his gloved hand. "I didn't want Lev to see this until we determined what it might be. It gives me a strange feeling."

Frowning, Marshall stepped closer so he could see the object under the terrible blue-toned lighting. He ought to ask around and acquire a candle for their own compartment. This light would give him night terrors if he lived under it for a week.

"A needle?" Marshall asked, bemused.

Benedikt changed the angle at which he was holding the thin stick of metal, pinching around its middle instead of its end. Now Marshall could see the rough cut at one of the tips, as if it had been snapped off something.

"A syringe needle."

"Maybe it was left there from the previous occupant?"

Benedikt stirred his tea. He had requested a wedge of lemon that bobbed in the dark liquid, swimming along the sides with each revolution of his spoon. The dining table in front of them was entirely covered in bits and bobs. Popov's wallet. His briefcase's contents. The train's paperwork regarding every trip he had made on the railway. With the hour nearing ten o'clock, most of the dining car passengers had retired to their own compartments, but there were still one or two dawdlers who ate their desserts or read their books under the soft glow of the chandelier at the bar. If they had to walk past Benedikt and Marshall's table, however, they gave a wide berth to the makeshift workstation.

Or maybe that was because of Lev, pacing up and down in the aisle beside the table, muttering under his breath as he deliberated headlines for his upcoming piece.

Benedikt let the boy do his own thing, turning his attention back to the clues in front of them—without the needle, of course.

"The attendants would have cleaned it away, or the provodnitsa would have seen it," he replied, keeping his voice quiet. "It wasn't well hidden at all. It was lying right on the carpet before I picked it up."

The most likely scenario was that the syringe needle had been flung there in a struggle. But how was it used? Where was the syringe itself? Benedikt couldn't wrap his head around it. There was no chance of getting an autopsy performed or the corpse examined unless the train stopped—and the whole point of this front as private investigators was to avoid the train's delay and reach Vladivostok as soon as possible.

"I suppose we can check for injection marks in the morning light," Marshall said thoughtfully. He tipped backward on his chair. It would serve him right if the chair legs suddenly snapped and he went sprawling on the floor. "Beyond that . . . what about motive?"

Lev was still pacing. The old woman sitting in the corner looked more and more concerned, and when Lev suddenly threw his arms up and made a cry of revelation, she hurried to mark her book, scuttling away from the table and retreating out of the dining carriage. With the boy too distracted to glance their way, Benedikt stretched his legs out under the table, hooking one foot around the rung on Marshall's chair and tugging him forward so he wouldn't fall. Marshall grabbed his ankle before he could pull it away.

"At least we confirmed that we have his correct name," Benedikt replied. He yanked his ankle once more, trying to get it back. Marshall, mischievously, held on tight. There was no indication in either of their voices of the battle going on under the table.

"Assuming his identification isn't forged."

"Sure. If anything is forged, though, I suppose we have much grander problems. His permanent address puts him in Moscow."

Marshall's grip started to slide higher. Benedikt used his other leg to kick, and with a silent protest, Marshall was forced to release him.

Let me love you, he mouthed.

Arrested for public obscenity, Benedikt mouthed back in warning.

"Yet he comes and goes often," Marshall continued aloud without missing a beat, gesturing to the log of Popov's past trips between Moscow and Vladivostok. "I don't suppose this was only a simple robbery from someone who had memorized his usual itinerary."

Benedikt flicked the leather wallet on the table, sending it from one corner to the other. "If it were, there wouldn't be any money left behind."

The dining car bounced. The chandelier above the bar made a tinkling noise, its glass beads jangling upon collision with one another. It was getting late. They still had six days, after all. Even Lev seemed to have run out of energy from his pacing, standing by the moss-colored wallpaper and mumbling to himself.

"I'll be damned if we can figure out a motive from this alone." Benedikt sighed, shaking his head. "Let's call it a night."

5

It was surprisingly soothing to sleep on a moving train. Benedikt didn't wake once through the night, not from the rumbling of the engine or the screeching of the tracks. Only when morning arrived and fellow passengers started to move along the passageway outside did he stir, catching snippets of complaints passing outside his door.

On any normal journey, the train would have been making stops today. Instead, passengers holding tickets for the nearest destinations would have to ride for another five days until Vladivostok.

It didn't sound like people were very happy about the announcement. Benedikt didn't particularly care about the other passengers grumbling as long as it served his purpose.

He eased out from underneath Marshall's heavy arm, moving carefully to avoid waking him. For a moment, it seemed Marshall had been roused, mumbling something about soup. Benedikt stopped, wondering if he ought to go fetch some soup, but then Marshall continued snoring, his crop of dark hair falling off his forehead and against the soft pillow.

Suppressing a smile, Benedikt hurried to get dressed in the half dark, the curtains blocking out most of the rising daylight. He only caught the barest glimpse of himself in the small mirror hanging from the wall before exiting the compartment, running a hand through his hair so he didn't have a yellow clump at the back of his head.

Benedikt nodded at the attendant standing guard outside the dead man's room.

"May I enter?"

The attendant, recognizing Benedikt as the investigator, moved aside, opening the compartment door. With the curtains drawn back in this room and the morning streaming bright, Benedikt made his second perusal quickly, not wanting to hover around the corpse for too long lest the metallic smell seep into his clothes. At least there was no bodily decomposition yet. In another day or so, it wouldn't only be the stench of murder, it would be the stench of decay.

"All right," Benedikt muttered under his breath. "Let's see."

He rolled up the dead man's sleeves carefully, examining his limbs for a site of injection. Stiffness had set in on the corpse, making it exceedingly difficult to move elbows or shoulders around as needed, but Benedikt tried his best. He prodded at the cold skin. Maneuvered around rubbery lines and rigid fingers.

Ten minutes later, he hadn't found anything of note, and he rolled Popov's sleeves back down in defeat. He went as far as to peer around the deceased's throat and jostle the murder weapon around, checking the skin beneath the clumps of dried blood, but there was no sign of a puncture wound . . . apart from the ink nib itself, of course.

Benedikt got to his feet. Wrinkled his nose at the body as if the man's death had been a personal slight against him. It might as well have been—this was supposed to be the *restful* part of his journey.

With a sigh, Benedikt exited the compartment and nodded to the attendant, letting him resume watch over the crime scene. He was deep in thought as he proceeded to the dining car, mulling over their next options.

"Good morning, Mr. Sokov."

Benedikt startled as he grabbed a muffin from the food cart, needing a moment to register where the loud voice was coming from and another moment to realize that he was the one being addressed.

Vodin was sitting at a table with a cup of coffee in front of him. His mustache was brushed very primly.

"Hello," Benedikt said plainly. "Can we question the passengers and attendants in soft-class today?"

An attendant pushed in a new cart of fruit. Vodin took a sip of his coffee.

"Not one for idle conversation, are you?"

Benedikt frowned. "What is this, high society?"

"Ah, touché." Vodin looked a little amused at Benedikt's curt attitude. He wasn't putting on a comedic act, though. This was just how Benedikt talked. "Of course—I will ask every passenger and attendant across the soft-class carriages to cooperate. Where is your investigation partner?"

Benedikt bit into his muffin. He didn't bother taking a seat when he would be done in a few seconds anyway. "Marshall is still resting."

"Late night?"

Benedikt's frown turned even deeper. "I suppose so. We sent Lev off around the time when we were concluding our work. It wasn't as late as it could be."

Vodin finished his coffee. He nodded, then wiped the milk foam from his mustache. "Speaking of my nephew, I will go wake him now. I hope he can sit in on the questioning."

"Of course." Benedikt stepped aside as Vodin got up. "We can start in an hour or so."

"Very well." Vodin tipped his black hat. For whatever absurd reason, he looked like he was barely holding back a laugh. "In the meantime, Mr. Sokov, you may wish to consult the mirror. Or not. Up to you. I will fetch my nephew."

The officer sauntered off. With immense confusion, Benedikt

leaned over the food cart, finding a reflective surface to peer into. This time, he looked at himself properly.

"Damn it, Marshall," he hissed, reaching for a cold spoon and pressing it to his neck.

Marshall was startled awake by the sensation of something cold thwacking him on the forehead.

"Ah, shibal—"

His eyes flew open, bewildered and groggy. Benedikt, or rather the fuzzy impression of Benedikt, was standing over him, holding what looked to be a metal spoon.

"Ow!" Marshall complained.

"*Ow?*" Benedikt echoed. He pointed to his neck.

Marshall blinked rapidly, clearing his vision. Now he could see Benedikt clearly, from his golden hair to his brown-gray, ambiguously dark eyes, to the faint bruise at the left of his throat, kissed into existence right before they went to sleep.

He grinned. "I was wondering when you would notice that."

"By God"—Benedikt rolled up his sleeves—"I'm going to kill you."

"Nooooo, we're trying to catch a murderer, not become one!"

"Too late!"

Benedikt clambered onto the bed, spoon raised. Marshall threw his head back and laughed, yanking his husband down and trying to avoid getting beaten to death by a spoon.

6

"Here is the passenger list for everyone in soft-class. The smaller section at the end is the attendants."

Vodin put a clipboard down onto the dining table. It was only two pages, listing the twenty or so passengers scattered on these four carriages. There were five attendants and one provodnitsa, making a total of seven service staff including Vodin himself. While Marshall chomped down on his apple—rather aggressively because he was trying to maximize the taste and his senses always got a little dulled while traveling—Benedikt picked up the clipboard and scanned through, making a noise at the back of his throat.

"I don't suppose you spot any names of already-famous criminals?" Marshall asked, leaning forward. They were seated on the same side of the table they had used for a workstation last night. Their suspects would sit for their interrogation on the other side, one by one.

"That would be rather convenient," Benedikt said. "Sadly, I do not."

"Damn. It was worth a try."

"A valiant effort, Mars."

Marshall thought so too. He took another bite of the apple, his gaze flickering up to the carriage doors as Lev pushed his way in, scuttling close to the table.

"Are we interviewing people today?" he whispered. "How very Sherlock."

"Let's get one thing clear," Benedikt said, waving for the kid to sit down. "*You* are observing. Don't go sticking your neck out. One of these people walking in today will be a killer."

Lev immediately nodded, looking as serious as a pallbearer. Even Marshall felt his stomach drop a little, swallowing his next bite nervously as Vodin peered out the doors of the dining carriage and waved for the first group of waiting passengers to get ready. This had been the very basis for their investigation. To deny the possibility of an escape, the train had not stopped, so whoever had stabbed a pen through Danila Andreyevich Popov's throat remained on board. They only needed to point the finger at whom.

"Ready?" Benedikt whispered.

Marshall threw the apple core into the trash can. "Ready."

The elderly lady who Lev had scared off last night was waved in first. The questions only served to get a better picture of who was where during the time of the crime, which meant plenty of passengers were ushered through and allowed to leave in minutes. *Where were you yesterday? Who was with you? Did you know the deceased? Did you see anyone near his room at the time of the crime?* Plenty of them could vouch for each other in the dining car, and as soon as they had that, it was incredibly unlikely they had anything to do with the crime.

"Stepan Maximovich Ivanov," Marshall greeted when the man came through the dining carriage doors. "A pleasure to see you again."

"If only it were under better circumstances," Stepan replied, settling heavily into his seat. He had a businesslike demeanor, his hands clasped in front of him as if he were preparing to listen to a proposal rather than attending a questioning.

"You were in your compartment at the time of the crime, yes?" Benedikt asked.

"I was."

"And your traveling companion?" Marshall asked. He scanned the passenger list. "Can Mr. Portsmith confirm your presence?"

"He was rather deeply asleep. Claimed to have desynchronosis because he had just traveled from London to Moscow."

Benedikt scoffed. "A mere two hours?"

"He is old. It is fair."

"Interesting."

Where Marshall trusted that he could rely on his own head and remember the details that emerged as important, Benedikt was taking notes on every passenger, a few sheets of paper pressed to his leg. He was scribbling quickly now.

"Mr. Ivanov," Benedikt said, "why didn't you come out when the provodnitsa screamed? You had been speaking to my partner only a few minutes prior, and you were in the next compartment."

"Oh, that has an easy answer." Stepan Maximovich pointed to his ears. "Cotton-wrapped wax earplugs. They gave them out when we fought in the war to muffle gunfire, and I have been using them for sleep ever since."

It did seem a little convenient. But there was nothing overly suspicious about wearing earplugs to sleep either.

"Did you know the deceased?"

"No."

"Did you witness anything peculiar regarding the deceased?"

Stepan shook his head. He inclined his head to Marshall. "Nothing save for the muffled argument, which we discussed together. I didn't catch any of the words exchanged, or else I might be of more use today."

They dismissed Stepan and summoned in the next passenger: his allocated traveling companion. When Mr. Portsmith came in, he only confirmed the same answers. Or rather, he first used broken Russian to say that he would be utterly useless for questioning because he couldn't speak the language, hopping out of the seat presumptuously as soon as he sat down.

"Mr. Portsmith," Benedikt said drolly when the man rose. "We speak English perfectly fine."

"Yes, don't go spreading rumors to the other foreigners traveling on board that we will go easy on them," Marshall added. "We have at least a dozen languages between us."

Mr. Portsmith blinked. He lowered himself back onto the chair slowly. "Oh. Oh, all right."

The questioning proceeded. Most were Russian, but there was one Frenchwoman. Another Englishman. Three Chinese passengers. The majority of suspects who came through could name one or two others who were with them at the time of Mrs. Kuzmina's scream. They all claimed to be unfamiliar with the deceased. Even if a few couldn't resist adding a barbed comment about missing their destination during the questioning, each passenger was largely cooperative, answering politely before being dismissed and allowed to return to their rooms. It made sense. If a murderer walked into questioning before a clue had been found or a suspect identified, it would be rather silly to stick their nose out and draw attention to their guilt.

Then the next man walked in, slamming the doors to the carriage, and Marshall almost jumped out of his skin in fright.

"This is ridiculous!" The loud bang at the entrance clearly wasn't enough. As the man marched his way over to the table, striding wide in a manner that looked like his gray trousers had caught on fire, he also slapped one of the dining chairs, sending it skidding against the wooden floorboards. "What authority do you have to be holding us like this?"

Marshall glanced over Benedikt's shoulder, peering at his notes. The passenger list identified this man to be Eduard Kozlov. There was no noted patronymic. *Oh dear*, Benedikt wrote under Eduard Kozlov's column, angling the paper when he felt Marshall's gaze so Marshall could read the English words.

"Actually"—Benedikt sounded perfectly unperturbed by the man's aggressive question—"when you purchased your ticket, you agreed to its conditions, and those conditions include the officer on board determining your passage."

Eduard Kozlov made an immediate sneer. "So who the hell are you two? Not the officer, clearly."

"If the train officer entrusts us with the proceedings, then we are your makeshift officers too." Marshall leaned his elbows on the table, lacing his fingers together. "Would you like to sit?"

"I would not. I would like to get *off* at my destination."

"Then I would recommend you answer our questions," Benedikt said, "because the quicker we find this murderer, the more likely it is that this train will resume its normal passage. Now, are you going to cooperate?"

It seemed that Eduard took that as his cue to depart. His nostrils flared, then he spun on his heel, kicking another chair before exiting the dining carriage.

"Surely it would be far too obvious if that turned out to be our killer," Marshall said.

"You never know." Benedikt had added 不肯合作 in his column of notes. *Unwilling to cooperate.* "Maybe the universe is giving us a break."

Marshall leaned closer. "Are you writing in Chinese?"

Benedikt started a new line, switching languages. 화났어 . . .

"I'm writing in everything but Russian," he replied. "Less chance of someone stealing my notes and understanding them."

"Yes, because I'm sure the killer will see vague remarks such as 'is angry . . .' and go on another scathing rampage."

"My Korean vocabulary is rusty, all right?"

Leaning over, Marshall plucked away the pen and added: 의자 찾어 ☺

Benedikt snorted. "Did you have to draw the sad face?"

"Yes. That poor chair."

The door to the dining carriage slid open again, bringing a new passenger. In stark contrast to Eduard, the girl who entered next only poked her head in first, cautious about interrupting. Marshall recognized her, though it took him a second to recall why.

"Vodin sent me through," she said.

"Come and sit," Benedikt prompted, taking his pen back and tapping it twice on Marshall's knee to tell him to get back on task. "This will be quick. You are . . ." He consulted the passenger list. "Yeva?"

The girl nodded, walking forward and sliding into the seat. She was wearing a pale green dress in a collared style that felt reminiscent of Shanghai, though perhaps cities spreading their fashion to each other was no big surprise. A silver necklace dangled outside the lace, its pendant engraved with an English letter *Y*.

"Yeva Mikhailovna, at your service." Her voice came quietly, not because of timidity, but merely as if that were her default volume.

"No family name?" Marshall asked.

"That is not so strange in this day and age," she answered easily.

Marshall supposed he had to agree. After all, his full name on this train ride was "Just Marshall."

"Are there any other passengers who can account for your whereabouts at the time of the crime, Yeva Mikhailovna?" Benedikt asked, probably writing her lack of surname into his notes too.

"That depends," Yeva answered. She smoothed a stray piece of hair away, pressing it back into her low bun. "When the provodnitsa screamed, I was alone in my own room drinking tea. But a few minutes beforehand, if that is when the crime occurred, you two saw me."

Benedikt looked up suddenly, surprised at the statement. He likely hadn't noticed, nor made note of the passageway encounter. Since Marshall was the one who had almost collided with her, he nodded easily, confirming the account.

"Did you know the deceased?" Marshall asked, picking up the questioning while Benedikt scribbled.

Yeva shook her head firmly.

"All right. Last question, and I suppose this is especially relevant since you were nearby. Did you see anyone suspicious at the time of the crime?"

For a moment, it seemed Yeva was about to shake her head again. Only then she paused, her brow furrowing in thoughtful contemplation.

"I was in a hurry to get back to my room, so I did not see anything," she said slowly. "But . . . around fifteen minutes earlier, I was also walking by to get some food. I heard arguing, and I think it may have been from the deceased's compartment."

No one seemed to have seen a guilty perpetrator go into the deceased's room, but everybody had heard the muffled argument.

"Chances are high," Marshall said. "Thank you very much for your help, Yeva Mikhailovna."

Yeva blinked. "You . . . do not want to know what the argument was about?"

Benedikt's chair creaked as he sat up straight. "You actually caught what was said?"

"Of course," Yeva said, appearing bewildered at any alternate possibility. "It was so loud. I didn't catch much because I thought it inappropriate to linger, but I did hear one command very clearly. He said, 'Don't you dare. Don't you dare put that in me.'"

In an instant, Marshall met Benedikt's eyes and knew they were thinking the same thing. Unless Popov was deluded enough to reason with a killer before they stabbed a weapon through his throat, it was likely that this occurred before the crime, and he was speaking about a syringe instead.

"Thank you, Yeva," Benedikt said. "Could you send the next passenger through on your way out?"

The sun was setting. Once the rapidly moving skies finished burning red and color seeped down the horizon like liquid from a wrung-out washcloth, another day would have passed upon the Trans-Siberian Express.

Marshall flipped through the encyclopedia in his lap, humming beneath his breath. They had left the overhead light off, still intent on soaking up the last of the sunset. While Marshall made a concentrated effort to browse through the thick tome he had retrieved from the dining carriage's corner library, his legs stretched out on the bed and his posture curled to put him close to the page, Benedikt was sitting on the floor instead with his sketchpad, leaning his head back on Marshall.

"I don't suppose drawing has given you a big revelation?" Marshall asked, cutting into the quiet.

"It has, actually," Benedikt replied in an instant. He shaded the grassy scene on his paper, then paused before adding a tiny cow to his field. "I have realized I need to draw more cows. They are very nice."

Marshall rolled his eyes, softly thumping Benedikt over the head.

"I meant about the investigation, Ben. We have a ticking time bomb."

"A time bomb, too? I thought we only had a dead body."

"You think you're so funny."

"You laugh at all my jokes, so whose fault is that?"

Marshall pushed the encyclopedia off his lap, then leaned over and put his hands around Benedikt's neck, pretending to strangle him. It was no fun, because Vodin would want his report in a few hours, and instead of experiencing joy at being a nuisance, Marshall moved so that his arms wrapped along Benedikt's shoulders instead, resting his head there as his thoughts raced. He had hoped the encyclopedia would have some sort of scientific method for determining the presence of chemicals in dead bodies. Even though Benedikt said that he hadn't found an injection site while checking the body again this morning, Yeva's claim about what she had overheard made it likely that the syringe had been used.

But the only interesting thing the encyclopedia had been able to offer him were facts about clouds. Which was nice, but irrelevant for his specific purposes. Maybe if they already had contact with Lourens, the old scientist would easily be able to offer a method of deduction. Except by the time they were in contact with him, one could only hope they had already solved this murder.

"Hey." Benedikt reached up to touch Marshall's arm, his tone turning earnest. "Don't fret so much. I am supposed to be the nervous one."

"We cannot both be the nervous one?"

"Absolutely not. That is far too many nerves in one marriage."

Marshall laughed. He tipped his head so that it was his cheek leaning on Benedikt's warm shoulder instead, the heat of skin emanating through the white cotton shirt Benedikt had changed into. There had been so many times in their childhood when he had wanted to do this. When his palms had practically stung in his craving for touch while knowing he had to rein back, knowing he couldn't risk crossing the line. Instead of stealing a kiss, he had gotten by with playful punching. Instead of touching Benedikt's hair when it shone painfully bright under the morning sun, he had leaped at his best friend, demanding to be carried on his back. Marshall Seo had grown up playing himself off as a joke; it was always easier to pretend that he didn't really mean something, to shrug a matter off and feign carelessness.

Benedikt, in the present, turned his head. "You're being awfully quiet, Mars."

Yet even when the rest of the world was fooled, Benedikt took him seriously. The last star could burn out and the oceans could dry to nothing, but Benedikt would be there, letting Marshall protest and fuss and grouse until his true face came out.

"I am only thinking," Marshall said. "About you."

"Good thoughts, I hope."

"Dirty ones, actually."

Benedikt rolled his eyes. Before he could respond, however, there was a muffled crash in the passageway outside, and then a yell of alarm. Both Marshall and Benedikt were up within seconds, knowing that there could only be so many reasons someone was yelling on a train with an active crime scene.

Marshall threw open the compartment door. His first instinct was to look left, in the direction of the dining carriage. When another cry sounded, he was almost surprised to discover it was from the right.

"Hang on, hang on," Benedikt warned before he could start in that direction. "What is it?"

A woman stumbled out of the washroom at the end of the carriage.

"I-i-in there," she stammered. "I only turned on the lights and . . ."

She had been among the passengers interviewed only hours earlier. Marshall couldn't recall her name, but he gave her a reassuring smile as he brushed by, saying, "Take a deep breath. I will have a look."

He stepped into the washroom. On the mirror, there was a message penned by a careful hand.

In dripping, crimson blood.

STOP LOOKING

7

"Okay, well, the good news is that it's not blood."
Benedikt swiped a finger against one of the Cyrillic
letters, taking off its tail. He rubbed the smudge against
his thumb and continued, "Oil-based paint, I would guess. It looks
very difficult to clean."

A sudden flash of light flared over his shoulder. Benedikt whirled
around quickly, then almost knocked into Lev, who had silently
approached from behind with his camera out.

"Oops," the boy said. "Don't mind me. Getting some pictures."

"Yes, I can see that," Benedikt said, sidling out of the way. His
knee nudged against the porcelain toilet bowl.

Alongside Lev's appearance, a group of passengers had also
gathered in the passageway, drawn by the woman's cry and curious
over what the hubbub was. A shelf of soaps had been knocked over
in her panic. It was collapsed sadly by the toilet bowl. While onlookers drew closer and tried to peer in, Marshall did his best to wave
them off from the door, saying that there was nothing interesting
here to see.

It clearly wasn't true—not when Lev had been let in to take his
photos.

"Mars," Benedikt called. "Come in. The rest of you outside need
to make some space in case the message here is poisoned."

There was no chance that someone would go mixing poison

into paint—because it would be a rather fruitless endeavor—but his warning did the trick. The passengers quickly scattered back, muttering about whether they were in danger and putting their handkerchiefs to their noses. It was only Mr. Portsmith who remained where he stood, poking his head into the washroom. He hadn't understood Benedikt when he spoke in Russian.

"What does that say?" Mr. Portsmith nodded at the mirror.

"Mr. Portsmith, please return to your compartment," Marshall replied, switching to English. "We must conduct an investigation here."

The old man huffed. "What a frightfully boring journey," he muttered. "I spent about ten minutes yammering to that Yeva girl at the samovar before realizing she didn't understand me. I can hardly get through to my traveling companion either, and now the only English speakers won't answer a simple question. . . ." He shuffled off, still grouching to himself.

Marshall stepped in through the door, finally having rid the passageway of onlookers.

"Why the washroom, of all places?" he wondered, eyes tracing the scene.

As far as train facilities went, the washroom size was rather generous, or at least enough so that Benedikt could stretch his arms wide and not nudge either of the deep green walls. Perhaps it was because the compartments didn't come with their own washrooms, unlike some other train designs. There was only one in each carriage that the passengers had to share for a full week. A shower attachment could even be pulled off the wall, though Benedikt didn't sense any dampness on the floor or see any water collected around the drain to signal its recent use. One bulb dangled on a string from the ceiling. The porthole window offered little but the fallen dusk outside.

"Other parts of the train are rather closely watched," Benedikt guessed. "The washroom is the only private place to leave a threatening message without being seen."

Stop looking. It was rather vague as far as threats went too. They could have gone for "You are next." Or even "I will kill again." But instead, it was an instruction regarding the investigation itself.

Fair enough, Benedikt thought to himself. Popov had been arguing with someone before his death. This had to have been a crime with a motive, a murder committed in answer for something he had done, or someone he had upset. Once he was dealt with, the problem was solved. There was a killer on board, but that killer probably wasn't a big threat anymore, unless someone *really* pushed them to act again.

Another flash of light. Lev was leaning right over the metal sink, getting close to the mirror.

"You keep him company and continue looking," Marshall said, stepping back into the passageway. "I will report to Vodin—I figure this message works in our favor."

"In your favor?" Lev cut in excitedly. "How so?"

Benedikt plonked two hands on the boy's shoulders and maneuvered him to face the mirror again. "Take your pictures promptly. I am getting itchy just watching you linger in here. It is in our favor because it means we're onto something."

Now it was just a matter of figuring out what. It wasn't as if any of the questioning had led to a pivotal clue. Neither Benedikt nor Marshall felt very assured about the direction of their investigation at all. They were two frauds groping around in the dark, and it seemed someone felt threatened enough to try to halt them in their tracks.

"Stay right here," Marshall said. He trekked off, pushing into the next carriage.

Lev turned back to the mirror's message. His camera shutter made a loud noise.

Then, before he could take his next picture, he decided to crouch down, angling up at the writing.

"Mal'chik," Benedikt said slowly. "What . . . are you doing?"

Lev looked away from his camera lens. He blinked his eyes innocently. "Getting this little fleck right here."

On days when Benedikt painted around their apartment in Moscow, he could be as careful as a surgeon and still Marshall would somehow walk into a splotch he had unknowingly dropped in the kitchen. It was always rather funny to listen to Marshall yell, though, startled that he had trod on something suspiciously wet and cold.

Benedikt traced down the mirror. Leaned in close.

At the base of the sink, right beside Lev's shoe, there was a smudged bit of red paint upon the linoleum floor. It hadn't entirely dried yet. The barest sheen of light bounced off the color.

"Lev, don't move," Benedikt warned.

The boy looked away from his camera again. "Huh?"

"Just stand there and keep taking your photos. I will return shortly."

Benedikt kept his eyes pinned down. He edged through the doorway carefully, then situated himself forward and reached for the wallpapered sides, gripping hard to maintain balance, as if that could minimize the amount of carpet he was stepping on.

He found the next phantom bit of paint right outside the washroom, where the linoleum met the navy-blue carpet. It would have been rather impossible to see the mark if he hadn't been looking closely. The dark color swallowed it right up.

He scoured the nearby carpet, looking and looking and looking. . . .

A cacophony of noise burst behind him, the carriage doors opening to bring Marshall, Vodin, and Mrs. Kuzmina. Marshall and Vodin were going back and forth rather forcefully about what more could be found in the investigation. The provodnitsa, meanwhile, was carrying a bucket of water and a cloth, likely heading for the washroom with the intention of cleaning up the mirror after Marshall had reported the scene.

"Hey," Benedikt called out.

Mrs. Kuzmina paused in front of the washroom. Marshall and Vodin, too, stopped mid-debate to glance over. In that one word, they had picked up Benedikt's concern—or perhaps it was more accurate to say that Marshall had picked up Benedikt's slight concern, and Vodin was only following the more visceral cues that Marshall was giving off.

Benedikt pointed to the door right beside the washroom. "Who occupies this room?"

"That room?" The provodnitsa set down her bucket. "Nobody. It is empty."

That was unexpected. And it didn't make any sense. Because if it was empty, why was there a third smear of the faintest paint smudge right outside the doorway, as if someone had made two long strides out of the washroom before disappearing right next door?

"Recently?" Benedikt pressed. Hearing his urgency, Marshall hurried over too. "Did someone move rooms?"

Mrs. Kuzmina reached into her pocket, pulling out her master key. "No, no. For this journey, there was no ticket holder for this room. See?" She put the key in, turning the lock and pushing on the handle. "Empty."

The door swung open. She flicked on the overhead light.

And though there were no sheets on the bed nor any clothes hanging on the wardrobe hangers, there *was* a single can of red paint sitting on the table with a wet brush lying beside it.

The train bounced. For a moment, no one said anything. Then, very seriously, Marshall demanded: "Is there any chance that we have a stowaway?"

The provodnitsa's mouth opened and closed. Disbelief turned her movements slow. "I don't know. I cannot imagine how."

This investigation was only getting stranger and stranger. Muttering a curse, Benedikt strode into the room, making a quick inventory of its contents. The compartment looked near identical to the others in the carriage. The curtains were drawn back. The one drawer beneath the wardrobe was ever so slightly ajar.

Out of instinct, Benedikt nudged it open with his foot. He didn't say anything. He let Vodin come into the room and start ranting about keeping track of where the keys were, the officer's pointer finger stabbing into his other palm forcefully as he instructed the provodnitsa on altering the lock on the door. When Marshall's gaze settled in his direction, Benedikt locked eyes meaningfully, then inclined his head at the drawer.

As naturally as he could, Marshall took a step toward the drawer, peering inside. Benedikt caught the exact moment Marshall saw it too: the smallest smattering of powder at the lower left corner. Anyone else might have mistaken it for dust. But Benedikt and Marshall hadn't grown up in one of Shanghai's most infamous gangs to make the same error.

Someone had been storing illicit drugs here.

Benedikt tossed the blanket forward, letting it flop onto Marshall's head. There were still a few stragglers who remained in the dining carriage, finishing their soup or taking their tea, so he switched to Chinese to avoid being understood.

"Dearest treasure of mine, we are supposed to be staying *awake*."

Marshall only groaned in response, letting the blanket stay over his head as he leaned up against the window and rested on the glass. Their investigation felt like it had been rewound and reset. Vodin had given them another twenty-four hours, seeing that *something* seemed to have pressed on the killer's nerve, though heavens knew what. They needed to get the officer a viable hypothesis soon so that he would allow the train to keep riding for the investigation. If they floundered too evidently, Vodin would bring in the police by tomorrow's nightfall.

Lev had gone to sleep. Marshall and Benedikt had assured him that the investigation wouldn't resume until tomorrow morning. In reality, they just needed as few people as possible knowing what they were about to get up to.

"The sweet endearment offers only the most infinitesimal reprieve to my poor eyes, which are dragging closed and heavier than stone, heavier than the heaviest substance known to mankind—"

Benedikt yanked the blanket off. He should have known better than to have tossed it forward to begin with, because of course Marshall would use it as a prop in his melodrama. He needed to take a different approach.

"You know"—Benedikt faked a sigh, folding the blanket carefully—"if you're tired, I can do this stakeout alone. It cannot be that hard to watch for movement throughout the night, and I can fend for myself if anything goes wrong. . . ."

Marshall's eyes flew open, his spine straightening. "I am not tired. Who told you that? Malicious slander and lies."

Immediately, Benedikt switched his countenance, thwacking a hand onto Marshall's shoulder. "All right, then. Look lively."

The last passenger didn't leave the dining carriage until well past midnight. Half an hour later, the last attendant finished wiping down the tables and also took his leave.

Benedikt turned his newspaper page, barely taking in the words. Marshall, meanwhile, leaned on Benedikt's arm with a thump. The stakeout had to be tonight; by tomorrow, news would surely start to travel about the empty room and the paint bucket, tipping the killer off about the discovery. Before the killer realized that Marshall and

Benedikt were onto the empty room, the two investigators were watching for movement in and out—either to confirm a stowaway or to eliminate the possibility and figure out if someone on board had merely gotten access. Besides, if there *were* a stowaway, surely they could not hide for more than a few hours at a time, especially if they didn't know that Benedikt and Marshall hovered nearby in anticipation.

In about ten minutes they would turn off the lights, then prop open the door into the nearest carriage and wait in the dark. If the killer decided to visit that room again, they would see.

Benedikt turned another page with his left hand, keeping his right arm still for Marshall. The chandelier over the bar flickered, as if it could sense that it was soon time to blink out.

"Do you think the syringe was for the same substance stored in that drawer?" Marshall asked suddenly. "Someone could be carrying both powder and liquid forms."

"I was thinking the same thing," Benedikt replied. "Maybe Popov was involved in a deal gone wrong."

Marshall made a thoughtful noise. "He seems more the business-man type than the criminal type."

"You never know."

"I suppose so."

By his tone, Marshall did not sound convinced. Benedikt wasn't too persuaded by his own words, in all honesty. There wasn't enough to work with. They had a dead body and a syringe at the crime scene. A threatening message on the mirror and a trail leading into an empty room that had previously held illicit substances. It gave Benedikt the feeling of holding two puzzle pieces that were supposed to slot together perfectly, only to find that the edges were disfigured and discolored. Where had the drugs gone? Why was the needle missing the rest of its syringe?

Benedikt sighed. Hearing the sound, Marshall draped an arm

over him, the motion firm. The physical warmth of fondness burned into Benedikt's heart at the gesture. A warm circuitry, spreading inside his whole body.

"Are you ready to sit in the dark?" Benedikt asked.

Marshall groaned.

"Ben?"

"Yes, Mars?"

"What if the killer is a ghost?"

". . . Did you snort something?"

"No, think about it. If monsters exist, what is stopping the undead from rising and moving around without us seeing them—"

"Ben?"

"Mm-hmm?"

"Phasing through walls is a possibility we need to be considering seriously. If some people can instantly heal their wounds and other people are being given inhuman strength, why can't there be *ghosts* that go invisible and—"

"Ben?"

"If this is another ghost theory, I might hit you."

"In an erotic way?"

"In a murder way, Mars."

"Maybe I should have been interviewing *you* as a possible killer."

"Mars."

"Yes, nae sarang?"

"When would I *ever* hit you erotically?"

"It doesn't sound that great to me either. Pretend I never gossiped about your cousin like this if he asks, but on the phone last month, Juliette said he was really into—"

At some point, Benedikt must have dozed off, because he jerked awake with a start, greeted by slashing lines of light cutting through the window. They were passing some small town. In seconds, its illuminated shape was left behind in the distance, and the dining carriage fell into a hazy black again. The color was different from a few hours earlier. It wasn't the heavy blanket of comfort when most people were asleep; it blushed with the faintest lightness of a dawn that waited an hour away.

Something was off. Benedikt glanced to his side and found only empty space where Marshall had been.

He jumped to the worst conclusion.

"Mars?"

His pistol had been hiding under the seat. Benedikt lunged for it now, the safety off in seconds as he pointed forward. A dozen scenarios flashed in his head: The stowaway emerging while Benedikt slept. The stowaway putting a bag over Marshall's face to muffle his yell. Maybe injecting him with something to knock him out. Slitting his throat and killing him before moving his body to guarantee he would make no sound. Benedikt hadn't seen any blood or a sign of a struggle, but as he inched through the dining carriage, inspecting the dark corners and waving his pistol in every direction, he didn't need any actual evidence to conjure up the image in his head.

He could hear his heartbeat going as loud as thunder in his ears. Somehow, above it all, he still managed to pick up the shuffle of movement at the end of the next carriage, where the compartments were.

He stepped over the threshold. The door was being held open by a large encyclopedia, the same one Marshall had been reading from, jammed in place to keep the mechanism from springing forward.

It was too hard to see. The passageway didn't have any natural light source. Benedikt could only rely on his eyes adjusting fast, using the barest illumination that streamed from the moonlit dining carriage, showing the dark carpet below his feet and each door that he passed. He trekked past his own door. Then, the room holding the corpse.

The sound was coming from the washroom. There was someone in there.

Benedikt lunged forward, his finger on the trigger.

"Whoa, whoa—"

And it was Marshall who reared back, his hands coming up.

"By God." Benedikt lowered the pistol, shoving the safety back on before putting the weapon away. "You scared the *hell* out of me, Mars!"

"I only needed the toilet!" Marshall said. In the low light, his eyes were wide and bewildered. "I didn't want to wake you!"

"You—"

Benedikt reached for him, arms tight around Marshall in an instant before he could protest. There was none: Marshall only embraced him in return, albeit with an air of confusion over why Benedikt was so worked up. He hadn't realized the amount of sheer adrenaline that had been coursing through him until his panic started to ease, until the roaring sound in his ears subsided and the breakneck *THUD THUD THUD* of his heart tried to sync up to Marshall's.

"You wake me," Benedikt said, pulling back a fraction. "When there is a killer on the loose and you're you and I'm me, you *wake* me."

"I'm sorry," Marshall breathed, seeming to realize where the panic had come from. After what they had gone through, it was only instinct to assume the worst at the earliest moment. Benedikt had lost him once. And it had been such a dismal and miserable world that he couldn't bear to do it again. "I'm sorry, Ben. I wasn't thinking."

Benedikt tried to pull himself together. Leaned in again until their foreheads were touching, breathed and breathed alongside the comfort and the ease that Marshall's proximity always offered.

"It's all right," he whispered slowly. "It's all right as long as I have you."

The sun was going to rise within the hour. With no result to their stakeout, there wasn't much point carrying it on until the bitter end. Soon, passengers would be rising and beginning their morning, and it wouldn't do to have them see the investigators milling about, looking tired and clueless.

Marshall seemed to come to the same conclusion, easing back slowly. Before Benedikt could take a proper step away, intent on pushing down the last of his distress and pretending it had never reared its ugly head, Marshall stopped him, his hands sliding to each side of Benedikt's face.

"Hey," he said quietly. His gaze was focused intently, wanting his words to be heard. "I love you, okay? I am never, ever leaving. I will tell you however many times you need to hear it. Just tell me when you need to hear it."

Benedikt's breath caught in his throat. "I know. I do know." He paused. Backtracked. "And by that, I meant to say I love you too."

A twitch of Marshall's lips. He breathed a laugh, then kissed him, as if it sealed in the assurance he had just made.

"We need sleep," Marshall decided. "Come on. It's a new day when we rise."

8

The time zone had changed again overnight, which meant when Marshall lifted himself awake and peered at Benedikt's wristwatch on the bedside table, he was rather confused. The display hands didn't match the high sun streaming through the window. The hours kept moving forward, and his watch couldn't catch up.

Benedikt was pushing the curtains back. Once he noticed that Marshall had stirred, he tossed something over, giving Marshall scarcely a second to register the object flying at him before his sleep-addled reflexes caught the apple.

"You are quite fond of tossing fruit at me, do you know that?" Marshall remarked.

"I'm feeding you, and you protest?"

"I was not protesting. I was fondly admonishing."

Benedikt snorted, reaching into the wardrobe. He shook out a towel. "I asked Vodin to check everyone's shoes in soft-class on the chance someone didn't clean the paint off."

Marshall dragged himself out of the blankets. God, he hated getting up. When his body was in stasis, it wanted to stay in stasis.

"He's doing that right now?"

"He is. He may find you to report back. In the meantime, I am off to rinse myself before *I* start smelling like a corpse."

Benedikt lightly thumped Marshall's head as he passed by,

walking out of the compartment and toward the washroom. He was so suave sometimes, never saying much but communicating with his touch. Marshall had learned by now that that was Benedikt's brand of affection, though he didn't think Benedikt had figured it out himself yet. A harmless bonk on the head may as well be a full-mouth kiss in Benedikt's mind.

"Up we get," Marshall muttered to himself, rolling right off the bunk and throwing himself onto the floor. The harsh landing snapped him into sudden alertness, finally giving him enough energy to stand up and shake some feeling into his arms. The apple was still sitting by the pillow, so he picked it up again and took a big bite. He didn't finish biting down—he kept his teeth lodged inside, holding the apple with his mouth so his hands were free to get dressed.

Ten minutes later, with his hair brushed back nicely and his spiffy clothes on, Marshall stepped out of the compartment and wandered into the dining carriage. It was nearly empty—only three occupied tables, passengers picking at their mystery meats and sauerkraut salads. Perhaps everyone else was still asleep too, unaccustomed to the changes in hour. Or perhaps they were hiding out in their rooms, either avoiding the murderer lurking on board or avoiding being caught as the murderer lurking on board.

An attendant offered him a drink, setting the glass on a coaster, an enormous block of ice taking up half the space inside.

"Mr. Marshall, a moment of your time?"

Vodin was striding through the dining carriage when Marshall turned around. Lev hurried at his heels, taking two quick steps for every one his uncle took. Where the kid looked bright and alert, the morning light wasn't kind to the officer, showing his tired eyes and the wrinkles in his collar. When Vodin drew closer to the bar and propped his elbow on the smooth granite surface, his appearance somewhat improved, gold color washed into his face by virtue of the chandelier lighting.

"If anything, it should be my pleasure to beg a moment of your time," Marshall replied. He turned to Lev and offered a casual two-finger salute. Lev returned the gesture enthusiastically. "How are the findings?"

"No paint on anyone's shoes, unfortunately," Vodin replied. "We asked passengers to volunteer their assistance, so you can imagine that if anyone boarded with more than one pair of shoes, it would be rather easy to hide the guilty set. For the sake of propriety, I do not think we are quite at a point of desperation to barge into each passenger's room to make a search."

No—that would be a waste of time when there were so many rooms in soft-class. The more effective route would be to narrow down the plausible suspects first before running searches of their compartments, but they didn't even have that yet.

Marshall kept his expression even. He didn't want the officer to think that they were struggling with this investigation. Or rather, he didn't want to confirm what Vodin might already be thinking.

Vodin patted dust off his sleeve. As Marshall stayed silent, mulling over his next suggestion, the officer continued: "Omsk is coming up along our route. The next stop, if we were running on a normal schedule. The police there will have tools to dust for fingerprints—"

"No, no, the moment we stop we will lose the culprit," Marshall cut in. "Don't you know how easy it is to run off? You have a few weak-muscled attendants standing as door guards, not militia soldiers. You cannot."

The attendant behind the bar frowned. "Hey."

Marshall grimaced. "Sorry. No offense. I am sure you are very lovely, but you have to admit"—he leaned over the bar, poking one finger at the attendant's thin arm—"you likely cannot go hand-to-hand with a murderer and win."

The woman sitting at the bar chuckled. The attendant frowned but didn't argue further, cleaning the glass in his hand and mumbling something inaudible under his breath about the possibility of hidden talents.

"Officer, we must collect handwriting samples," Marshall continued. If one branch of investigation didn't look like it was offering any results, he had to keep throwing different options at Vodin, give him the impression that something would be found. Though Marshall would be plenty pleased if they truly found something, his first priority was to keep the train running so they could get as close as possible to Vladivostok.

"Handwriting samples?" Vodin echoed.

"To match the threat written on the mirror," Lev supplied before Marshall could, sounding like it was the most obvious thing in the world. "It's the first rule of investigating. We could start narrowing down who wrote it."

The boy lifted his chin high. He glanced at Marshall, seeking approval, and Marshall immediately stuck both his thumbs high in the air. Lev beamed.

"I see." Vodin pushed off from the bar. He tapped the surface, considering, then nodded. "All right. Lev, you can help me then. Let's fetch the papers in my compartment."

Vodin ushered Lev away, giving Marshall a weighty look over his nephew's shoulder. It seemed to warn him that he needed to work fast—at the very least, have some new findings to report back while Vodin collected the passengers' handwriting. The door closed after him. The dining carriage returned to its usual procession of activity.

"Another drink?" the attendant asked. His tone sounded a little snootier after Marshall's comment about his weak muscles.

Marshall shook his head. He picked up his first drink, only half-consumed. "I am off to sit. If there are any more of those pastries at the back, though, do bring some for me."

He had his pick of seating, settling at a table in the corner, right beside the library shelves. The decor in the dining carriage gave the impression of an old manor house, and the unlit candelabras dotting each windowsill only accentuated the ambience. Just as Marshall was leaning toward the closest one, wondering if the wax was real or merely for appearances, someone cleared their throat from behind him, and he reared away, pretending to have only been stretching his neck.

"May I join you?" Stepan Maximovich Ivanov asked. His eyes were wide, as usual.

Marshall gestured to the free chair. "I would never decline company."

"Ah, you are better than I am." Stepan settled down, dropping into the chair before setting his cup of coffee on the table. A few drops spilled over the side. The man grimaced, but otherwise didn't fuss before using a thumb to swipe the liquid away from the saucer.

"So," the man continued. "Private investigation. How did you get into the field?"

Great question. Marshall wondered that himself sometimes. He supposed he could recount the series of events that had set him here today. Somehow, though, he figured it didn't make an appropriate story to describe his beginnings as a bastard child living in the Chinese countryside with his Korean mother, which led to joining the White Flowers upon her death, which led to his place beside the ruling Montagov family. Officially, he had been a gangster running their errands. Unofficially, he had been part troublemaker, part detective, part adviser—depending on the day and what new troubles stirred up in the underground empire. He'd had plenty of opportunity to develop private investigation skills.

"The way it always starts," Marshall replied, circling around the question. "A morbid curiosity as a child."

Stepan tapped his spoon against the side of his coffee cup. He bounced up and down once in his seat, in the manner of a chuckle.

"Are you very far from those days? You barely look old enough to be working."

"Very funny. I have been told I have a youthful glow."

After those early years on his own, fending for himself and trying to walk in an orderly line that didn't teeter entirely into oblivion, Marshall was used to a world where that was the norm. Shanghai was a beating, thriving world of opportunity at any stage. Heirs were primed to take over criminal networks at eighteen. Children ran messages into enemy territory because they were quicker and more agile when avoiding bullets.

"There is great benefit in that." Stepan sipped his coffee. He grimaced, face morphing in silent complaint over the bitter taste. "You get old and suddenly you can no longer flash a handsome smile to solve a problem."

Marshall snorted. "I don't think a handsome smile is going to help with this problem at present."

Stepan made a noise of agreement. He leaned back in his chair. Crossed one leg over the other. That perpetual look of surprise he always wore narrowed a minute amount, transforming into consideration.

"It is not going well?"

"Oh"—Marshall backtracked, not wanting to reveal too much—"it is going as it should. But wouldn't it be easier if there were shortcuts?"

"I imagine there must be a vast amount of information to cover. There is so much to look into regarding the deceased's work alone, never mind his personal life."

Marshall didn't quite register the full impact of that statement before he was already nodding along. Two seconds later, his nod halted mid-movement, and he tilted his head instead.

"Popov's work?" he asked. "I am not sure if I know what you mean."

"Oh?"

There was something very interesting about that one syllable. Because Stepan's tone of voice sounded confused, but when he met Marshall's gaze head-on, there was no sense of confusion there. Either his large, owl-like eyes were prone to going dull, or he had spoken on purpose so that Marshall would pick up on this thread of questioning.

Why?

"I wasn't aware you didn't know," Stepan clarified. That was a lie, Marshall decided immediately—the man stressed all the wrong syllables in his sentence as he feigned shock.

"The deceased wasn't around for very long; there was hardly time to offer information about his line of work," Marshall said. "No one on board has made his acquaintance prior to the journey either."

"The deceased was not around for very long, but for some time nevertheless." Stepan's attention moved behind Marshall, searching left and right. Marshall didn't know what the middle-aged man was looking at until he rose up and shuffled toward the library shelf, tapping a hand atop the row of encyclopedias before stopping at the white-spined books on the row below instead. "I had a conversation with him shortly after we boarded. He said he worked in pharmaceuticals."

Ten thousand different thoughts flew through Marshall's head at once. *Pharmaceuticals.* Something was starting to click together. Something at the very edges of what he was capable of grasping— but something nonetheless.

"Why didn't you mention this during questioning?" Marshall asked. "It feels like critical information."

"Why, I thought it was information that would have been discovered in his belongings already!" Stepan slid out one of the volumes, then brought it over to the table. When Marshall glanced at the front cover, he realized it was a telephone and address book, its pages as thin as whiskers, flopping under its own weight. THE MOSCOW DIRECTORY, it read. "He would be listed in here, I am certain. Now, don't go accusing me of withholding this when I am finding it for you."

"I wouldn't dream of it," Marshall said. Suspicion churned in his gut, but it didn't add up. There was nothing about Stepan's suggestion that seemed intended to throw the investigation off the right scent. Marshall didn't even have a scent to begin with. And yet Stepan had mentioned it for some purpose.

"All right. Excuse me now, I must catch up on sleep." Stepan rapped his knuckles on the directory. "The infernal sunlight woke me up too far early this morning. Best of luck, detective."

Just as Stepan was striding out of the dining carriage, Benedikt was striding in. The man offered a tilt of the hat in greeting, and Benedikt returned an expressionless nod. The door closed. Marshall immediately indicated for Benedikt to hurry closer, his motions furious.

"Where's the fire?" Benedikt asked, sliding into the seat Stepan had just departed from.

Marshall started to flip through the directory. It was organized by personal listings in the first three-quarters, then businesses and organizations at the back.

"Come closer."

Benedikt frowned. He pulled his seat over, looking more intently at the pages now. His hair was still wet, the ends slick against his neck. "What is it?"

"Nothing, I haven't found anything yet." Marshall paused, taking a moment to run through the Russian alphabet in his head. "Pharmaceuticals" would be nearer the end. He continued flipping. "I merely like your smell."

"And yet I'm the one who keeps getting accused of killer tendencies." Despite his words, Benedikt looked quite pleased. He subtly turned his nose down, sniffing his white shirt collar as if he wasn't sure what he smelled like. The train soap was horrific; he had brought his own, the same one he used in Moscow. Sea salt and pine wood. Charred at the edges like it had been dusted with warm smoke.

"Stepan Maximovich just told me that our dead man worked in pharmaceuticals."

Benedikt dabbed the back of his hand against his temple, taking away a drop of water before it could seep from his hair. "And he knows this because . . . ?"

"There was a brief conversation after departure, allegedly. I can't imagine how it came up, but it would be an awfully bizarre thing to lie about."

"Strange that he didn't mention it during questioning."

Marshall slapped the table. "That is exactly what I said!"

"Unless," Benedikt continued slowly, still chasing the same line of thought, "this information is something he already knew before he boarded the train, and he is trying to aid the investigation without coming off as a suspect."

The directory was now open to a page listing businesses involved with pharmaceuticals, starting with the research companies. There was Laboratory Ten, and Mercury Coats Research, and . . .

"Do you think Stepan Maximovich knows more than he is telling us?" Marshall asked. He turned the directory in Benedikt's direction, showing him one of the listings. There were two addresses side by side, one primary establishment in Moscow and one secondary in Vladivostok. Above the listing information, however, there was a single company name, claiming ownership to both establishments.

POPOV'S PHARMACY

"So our victim was the founder of a pharmaceuticals research company."

Marshall shook the directory vigorously. "We need to interview everyone again."

9

"Do you take any medicines?"

No one who sat down for questioning knew how to answer. Or rather, they would blink, trying to comprehend the relevance of the topic, then answer hesitantly—which Benedikt hoped meant they were caught off guard just enough not to lie.

"Sleeping pills, I suppose," Portsmith said.

"I have high blood pressure." Mrs. Kuzmina massaged her temples while she spoke. "Do you want a list of all my medicines?"

"Vitamins," Yeva Mikhailovna answered. "My husband tells me I need to keep my bones strong."

"I do not." Stepan kept an innocent expression. "Only the occasional painkiller."

By nightfall, they had made an abundance of scribbles on the passenger list, having questioned every person in soft-class but one: Eduard Kozlov. He had stayed in his compartment, refusing to show up.

Benedikt looked up as Marshall returned to the table holding two plates in his hands. He had asked the attendants for a quick dinner so that they didn't collapse while investigating.

"What is that?"

"Don't be fussy," Marshall replied. It didn't go over Benedikt's head that he deliberately did not answer.

"Veal?" Benedikt guessed, even more wary. He picked up a fork and prodded the side of the meat. Though it was smothered with brown gravy, the whole dish colorless, part of the meat fell free as soon as he nudged the fork against it, its quality dry and hard.

"Eat, Ben."

"Must I? Which of the attendants is doubling as the cook, because I would really like a word with—"

Marshall forked a piece into his mouth, shutting him up. The food didn't taste any better than it looked. But sustenance was sustenance, so Benedikt chewed obediently, trying not to make a face.

"How are our findings looking?" Marshall asked, leaning over to peer at the passenger list. "I am shocked that Vodin has such a long list of medications."

"I suspect he's had some sort of surgery recently," Benedikt said.

Marshall tilted his head. He had the sort of face that was loud about his confusion even if he didn't say a word; nothing could be concealed in the dip of his brow when he scrunched his forehead, nor in the way his lower lip would stick out just a little if he was trying to add something up but couldn't get it to fit quite right.

"He is always ginger with his left shoulder." Benedikt had noticed it on that first day when Vodin didn't lean his body into the door to leave but rather opted to push his hand forward. "Yet his handshake with his right hand is perfectly firm. It would make sense with why he's taking these medications."

"Wooooow." Marshall drew the exclamation long. When he propped his chin on his hand, his dark eyes were practically twinkling, light pouring from his smile. "You sound just like a real detective."

Benedikt pointed his fork at him. If he didn't warn Marshall off being so dramatic all the time, Benedikt was going to develop an ego sooner or later. Even though his fork-waving was a clear warning, Marshall only stuck his tongue out to lick the gravy off the utensil.

"You volunteered our services precisely because we have the qualifications."

"I suppose that is true. How do you feel about actually going into private investigation after this? We might make more money than education."

"Mars," Benedikt said dully. "You would *hate* that."

"I love saving the day."

"You couldn't be patient to save your life."

Marshall had been caught out. "Then educating children it is." He took a bite of his own food, chewed thoughtfully, then swallowed and said: "You know what else, though . . . If Vodin has a weak left shoulder, we also know for certain he is entirely innocent in all this."

Benedikt arched an eyebrow.

"Why do you say that? We have no reason to think Vodin did it, sure, but we can't entirely rule out any suspect." He wiped a single drop of sauce off Marshall's chin. Such a messy eater. "We should even suspect the provodnitsa: she was the first person Popov was rude to, after all."

That was the first rule of solving any murder, according to the novels, wasn't it? The culprit was never who the detective expected it to be. The final answer was always supposed to add up at the last minute once they had found some sort of revelatory piece of information. Even if it would make no sense for the officer in charge to have something to do with the murder, they couldn't discount anything.

But then Marshall said, "We can definitely rule him out." He set down his fork and picked up another utensil: the blunt knife. He flipped it around in his hand, the blade moving across his fingers with the practiced ease of agility, and stopped it when he made a fist. "Remember the cut on Popov's forehead?"

"Of course."

Slowly, Marshall made Benedikt set his utensil down too, then mimed attacking him with the knife. He was still making a fist around the knife, but instead of pressing the dull blade forward, he used the other end, drawing his elbow outward. Its metal grazed across Benedikt's skin, running a cold line from his temple to the center of his forehead.

"The cut was thickest by his right temple and thinner as it moved inward. He was hit like this: a backhanded smack of the coat stand from a left-handed grip."

Benedikt frowned. He reached for Marshall's hand, prying the blunt knife out of his grip and swapping it into his right hand instead, which was usually his dominant grip.

"I don't see why it couldn't have been like this." Benedikt, with his hands wrapped around Marshall's, pulled the proper end of the knife toward his temple and moved the arc inward.

"You're so silly," Marshall said with amusement. "Because it was a long coat stand, Ben. If someone was holding it with their right hand, it wouldn't require any need for this awkward movement. Look at how much my wrist is bent to create the angle. They would just"—Marshall shook his hand free, then tapped the dull knife directly onto Benedikt's forehead—"do this. Big smack."

It did make sense. It was impressive deduction, the stuff of real detective work. Benedikt nodded appreciatively. Marshall would know the gesture was the same caliber of admiration as his prolonged *Wooooow*.

"Should we look for someone left-handed then?"

"Not necessarily. In moments of panic people can pick up weapons with any hand. I suppose it only means anyone who cannot hit hard with their left is ruled out."

Benedikt picked his fork back up. Ate a bit of the terrible meat. "This . . . really doesn't narrow it down by much, does it?"

Night proper was settling heavily around the train. They were three days in, so their surroundings had turned into mountain ranges and snowy riverbeds. The Ural Mountains had been left behind in the daytime. The terrain had turned rougher since then, but it was nothing unrecognizable. The farther they pressed into Siberia, the sparser the scenery would turn. After Lake Baikal, even the stops that the Trans-Siberian Express would usually make grew farther apart. If they could just hold out until then, maybe they had a greater chance of pushing all the way into Vladivostok.

As if hearing Benedikt's thoughts, there was a rumble of commotion from the passageway outside the dining carriage. Unlike other times, however, this commotion sounded celebratory, and Benedikt slowly got to his feet, curious to see what the matter was.

He took a step toward the door. The train bounced under his feet. Was he imagining the slowing speed . . . ?

"We are stopping!" a passenger crowed, sticking their head into the dining carriage.

Benedikt whirled around. Marshall's horrified expression mirrored his own.

"Absolutely *not*," he declared, hurrying forward.

"We are only refueling. You do not have to worry."

Vodin waved for Benedikt to take a step back, looking concerned at the combative stance he had adopted. They had practically ambushed the officer as soon as he walked through the door. Benedikt shuffled slightly, inhaling deeply so he could lower his voice a sensible amount. Marshall squeezed his elbow, noting his tension. They stood in the passageway of the last soft-class carriage, right beside the guarded door that led into hard-class. In the search for answers, Benedikt had charged through all the carriages looking for Vodin, only to be stopped at the barrier by the attendant and told that he was speaking to the officers at the rear. Since those officers couldn't come forward, only Vodin received signal communication from the engineer driving the train at the front in the locomotive cab.

"But the doors need to remain *closed*," Benedikt emphasized. "The moment this train stops, it is an opportunity for escape."

Right on cue, the train came to a complete halt, pulling up to Novosibirsk-Glavny Station. A whistle of steam howled into the night. Since one of the nearby compartments had its door propped open—its passenger napping casually on the bed with no care for the conversation in the passageway—Benedikt could see flashes of the station through the compartment window. A few streetlamps lit the night scene. The station's turquoise green walls were an imposing sight, bright alongside the mounds of winter snow stacked at its sides.

It suddenly felt strange for the floor to be unmoving under his feet. He had gotten too used to the constant sensation of momentum. The world at rest felt like an unnatural state, some deviation from what was supposed to be routine.

"Don't worry. The people at the station will handle the task at the locomotive, so there is no need for anyone to step foot outside the train. We will be in Novosibirsk for no longer than twenty minutes. Like I said, there is nothing to be concerned about." Vodin looked around. "Where's Lev?"

"Here!"

The boy scampered out from another compartment clutching a lined piece of paper in his hands. "I think that is everyone's handwriting. We had a very pleasant chat about ink pens."

"Did you now?" Vodin peered at the paper, giving an approving nod. "Be a dear and take my satchel from me, would you? My shoulder is getting quite weak."

Lev hurried to ease the bag off his uncle's left arm. Benedikt cast Marshall a quick look. He had been correct about his guess.

"All the samples are in there," Vodin said. "The only one who wouldn't offer one was . . . Lev, what was his name again?"

"Eduard Kozlov," Lev supplied eagerly.

"Right, right. He was rather difficult about showing his shoes too. On this there was no answer at his door."

"Maybe we will have more luck trying," Marshall suggested. "Which is his compartment?"

Lev sidled closer to his side. "I can direct you there. I remember."

"Yes, you do that, Lev." Vodin was already gesturing for the attendant to step aside again so he could return to the hard-class carriages. "I have some further matters to sort out for hard-class, but keep yourselves busy. I will reconvene with you once the train is moving along."

He pushed out of the carriage. Lev bounded into action, exclaiming, "Follow me!" and charging in the other direction.

"We only ever seem to have terrible luck on trains," Benedikt muttered, meaning only for Marshall to hear his words.

"That's not true," Marshall replied brightly. "Our last trip into Zhouzhuang went perfectly fine."

"Our last trip, for Roma's birthday?" Benedikt asked, unsure if Marshall was being serious or pulling his leg. "In 1929? When our train halted on the Chinese Eastern Railway before our destination? Because the Soviet Red Army *had started fighting the Chinese*?"

Marshall winced. "It was a small skirmish. We transferred into Harbin smoothly."

"The Soviets detained almost every Chinese person in the Russian Far East! We were this close to putting a bag over your head to hide you from view in case they asked for your papers!" Benedikt put both his hands on Marshall's aforementioned head, steering him forward faster as they walked. "We all need to relocate before Sino-Soviet relations turn wholly foul and travel becomes unmanageable. I'm going to get early heart failure otherwise."

"I feed us too many healthy meals for you to get early heart failure."

At once, Benedikt moved his left hand so that it clapped over Marshall's mouth instead, keeping him quiet as they proceeded into the third carriage. "Nonsense. I could be a medical marvel."

"It's this one," Lev announced up ahead. He waited for Benedikt and Marshall, bouncing on his toes patiently in the middle of the carriage passageway. The floor remained stationary beneath them, but a low vibration was traveling along the carpet, shaking with the rumble of fuel being pumped into the engines.

Benedikt, becoming a professional again, removed his hand from Marshall's mouth as they stopped outside Eduard Kozlov's compartment. He straightened his posture. "Is Mr. Kozlov in there?"

"I think I hear something." Lev pressed his ear to the door. He listened for a moment, only looking curious, but then his expression flashed into confusion. "Actually, I hear a *lot* of rustling."

"Mr. Kozlov, if we could have a moment of your time." Marshall leaned forward to knock, his knuckles coming down on the compartment door. While he kept his tone nice, asking for cooperation, Benedikt mimicked Lev's position and leaned closer to determine exactly what he was hearing.

It wasn't just rustling. That sounded like the window being pushed back.

"Oh, *shit.*" Benedikt slammed his shoulder against the door without warning, scaring Lev and Marshall. "Stand back, stand back!"

He tried again, harder. The door flew open.

They were just in time to see Eduard Kozlov climbing through his compartment window while clutching a briefcase. A beat later, he slipped down the side of the train and into the night.

10

"Hold on! Benedikt!"

Too late. Before Marshall could shout another warning, Benedikt had shot forward in chase, shoving a foot onto the side of the bunk bed to push himself up and clambering onto the windowsill. Quick as a flash, he squeezed himself through too and jumped out on Kozlov's tail.

"*Why*," Marshall whined. Still, he didn't dawdle. While Lev stood there in shock, Marshall conducted the fastest scan of Eduard Kozlov's compartment. He spotted a key lying on the bedside table. On the desk was an advertisement flyer with thick, dark numbers scribbled over the top, as if someone had been trying to balance an account. Marshall didn't have the time to take a better look, but on mere first glance, he did think the flicked ends resembled the letters on the mirror.

"Lev, listen carefully." Marshall picked up the flyer and shoved it at the boy. "Find your uncle. Have him signal to the engineer to wait for us. We will return on board."

With that, Marshall ran for the window as well, hauling himself onto the sill and taking a flying leap out. The landing was rough on his ankles, but it was nothing he couldn't quickly recover from. He searched the night and caught sight of two figures. The train had stopped a bit farther along the tracks, overshooting its usual position; Kozlov seemed to be running for the station, which meant they were moving parallel to the carriages.

Think. Think fast.

Marshall sprinted forward. He couldn't think of anything. Was the station even open at this hour? Would there be other trains coming, or had they stopped running for the night?

"Mars!" Benedikt yelled from ahead.

Marshall jolted. How had Benedikt even known he was running after him? He was a considerable distance away.

"Get ready!"

"Ready?" he bellowed back. "For wha—"

With a whip-fast motion, Benedikt flung something, and Kozlov tripped, dropping his briefcase. Benedikt caught up to him in that quick tumble, diving to secure him in place, grappling in the dirt. Kozlov tried to punch up; Benedikt ducked fast and yanked his arm behind him.

Marshall felt around in his pockets.

Where is the gun, did it get put away this morning, oh wait, there it is—

Just before Kozlov could squirm his way out, Marshall drew onto the scene, pistol pointed. Slowly, Kozlov signaled that his hands were not going to move, staring at the barrel between his eyes. A single lamp at the side of the station lit their surroundings. Enough to catch every expression from the culprit held down in front of them, but not enough to differentiate the clumps of snow from the puddles of mud three paces away.

"Goddamn, it's *cold*," Marshall huffed. His breath was near opaque, blowing clouds with each word. Novosibirsk was already prone to below-freezing temperatures in the winter, but the snowfall earlier in the day had locked a frigid sensation into the air. Standing out here without a coat felt much worse than it needed to be. At least there was no wind.

"Speak quickly," Benedikt said, still keeping Kozlov in his hold. "How did you know Danila Andreyevich Popov, and what was your reason for killing him?"

"For crying out loud," Eduard Kozlov said. Then, to Marshall's utter surprise, the fight left him, the snarl disappearing from his expression and his shoulders slumping inward. Benedikt blinked rapidly, looking uncertain if he ought to keep holding onto him.

"I didn't kill him. I have no clue who he is. I only wanted to get out at Sverdlovsk, and now I will get punished for running late without a thing to show for it."

He . . . what?

"The message, though," Marshall guessed. "That was you. This whole investigation is messing with your plans."

Eduard Kozlov nodded. "I am no killer. I am only a product runner who cannot afford to make a seven-day journey when I was only supposed to be on that train for two."

Now Marshall knew how to make sense of this. The illicit substances in that empty room. He would bet that Kozlov had moved them into his own compartment when he saw searches being performed, afraid that the officer would stumble onto something.

His eyes darted to the side, where Kozlov's briefcase had fallen. If they opened it to look inside, they would surely find it filled to the brim with the same substance.

"Christ." Benedikt let go of him suddenly. "Gang activity?"

Kozlov looked hesitant to answer. "Well . . ."

That was a yes.

"So the syringe isn't yours?"

This time, Kozlov's hesitation was one of confusion, his brow furrowing as he gingerly got himself upright again. "What syringe?"

Benedikt cast a sidelong glance at Marshall. Marshall grimaced in response.

The illicit drugs on board had had nothing to do with Popov's pharmaceuticals work. The syringe found in his room had had no relation to the smuggling that was going on concurrent to the murder, one carriage away.

"You may go, Mr. Kozlov," Benedikt decided. "We believe you. Get to where you were needed before you are punished further."

Kozlov seemed like he couldn't believe what he was hearing. "I can . . . go?"

"We can say you ran off and we couldn't catch you." Marshall shrugged. He and Benedikt knew what it was like to belong to a larger network, moving at the whims and demands of the people above. They could hardly fault how some needed to make a living. The blood on their hands was thick and plentiful when it came to criminal behavior. At least Kozlov wasn't responsible for the actual crime they were investigating.

Kozlov nodded, picking up his briefcase and taking a few steps back without turning around, just in case it was a trick. The train, meanwhile, howled into the night with another whistle of steam, and then Benedikt and Marshall were too distracted anyway to watch Kozlov leave, because the wheels were suddenly groaning on the tracks, moving the train forward.

"Oh, no no no," Marshall exclaimed. "Is it moving—?"

A small head poked out the window from the soft-class dining carriage, a vast distance away from where Benedikt and Marshall currently stood. Though it was hard to see anything more than a vague outline, given all the lights were clustered near the station, the voice was easily identifiable as Lev's.

"*Mr. Sokov! Mr. Marshall! I can't get communication through to the engineer! Run for the last freight carriage! I can make them pause at the next stop!*"

The train was already speeding up. At once, Benedikt and Marshall sprang forward—Marshall cursing under his breath and Benedikt intently watching the last carriage.

"Ben, we can't get in."

"Yes, we can," Benedikt said. "I see the latch. We only need to get it open."

They drew up alongside the last carriage, running at a speed that kept them at pace with the train. In seconds, though, the train would accelerate and leave them in the dust. It didn't seem possible to act that quickly.

"Pistol!"

Marshall tossed his gun over. Benedikt caught it smoothly, then shot the latch, sparks of silver cascading down the tracks as metal struck metal. The freight carriages were very different from the passenger carriages—nothing more than a very large sliding door that almost resembled a barn entrance. There were no stairs that took a person up, so when Benedikt slammed his fist onto the freight door and slid the heavy metal open a fraction, he threw the pistol in first, then dared to get as close to the screeching wheels as he could before hauling himself into the carriage.

The train was accelerating. Marshall was lagging behind.

"Mars! Come on!"

"Wait, wait, wait, I don't know how to pull myself up—"

Benedikt gripped the side of the freight door, then stretched his arm out, leaning half his body into the night. For a moment, it seemed that he wouldn't be able to reach Marshall, that the train was pulling too far ahead and the distance was growing too great. But as soon as Marshall reached forward, Benedikt got a grip on his wrist and hauled him in without a second to spare, both of them collapsing onto the floor of the freight carriage.

"That was damn *close*," Benedikt panted into the dark.

Marshall was still lying on top of him, but neither made any effort to move, too busy trying to catch their breath. The dark freight container was crammed with boxes, if the cardboard corner nudging into Marshall's shoulder was any indication. The train resumed full speed again. It bounced once on its tracks. The door had slid itself shut, keeping out the arctic temperature outside.

Marshall grasped Benedikt's face, smacking a dozen kisses anywhere he could.

"You are my hero," he declared. "Plucked me right up like a mighty rescuer."

Benedikt spluttered a laugh. Though Marshall couldn't see him properly without any light, he felt Benedikt's grip tighten around him, their limbs still entangled.

"I would reroute the train with my bare hands before I left you behind," he said matter-of-factly.

"How very romantic."

"I know." Benedikt nudged his chin closer, taking a proper kiss. The train floor was dusty, the steam engine howled like a wolf's call around them, but Marshall leaned into the embrace without caution, taking the few seconds when they could pretend that the rest of the world had fallen away. Benedikt kissed like he painted: with consuming, frantic inspiration before slowing down to find the details and pinpoints.

They drew apart reluctantly. The door thudded to their side, its broken latch swinging back and forth against the exterior, beating out a rhythm.

"The next stop is Krasnoyarsk," Marshall said, picturing the approximate map of the Trans-Siberian Express. "It could be a full day before we arrive and get out of this freight container."

Benedikt sighed. He tilted his head back with a thud, and given he was still lying on his back, it created a rather painful-sounding impact with the wall behind him.

"Start thinking hard, then," Benedikt said. "Because we are right back to square one."

11

It wasn't until after a new night fell, a whole daytime passing at a snail's pace, that the train started to slow again. Five minutes later, it came to a complete stop.

"Are you two alive in there?"

The door thudded open. Benedikt sat up, nudging Marshall out of his doze. Only moonlight illuminated the station's surroundings as Vodin hauled himself into the freight carriage, peering around as if he had expected to find something other than two pseudo-investigators crammed up with the boxes, covered in day-old dust.

"Debatable," Benedikt replied wryly, checking his wristwatch. "Have we arrived in Krasnoyarsk?"

"Yessir." Vodin crossed his arms. He sounded slightly winded from his brisk walk over from soft-class—he must have hurried out as soon as the train stopped, because it had been less than thirty seconds before his appearance. "Did we get an escapee?"

Benedikt grimaced, ending the back-and-forth volley of questions. He got himself onto his feet, dusting off his trousers to put some semblance of respectability into his appearance. Marshall, on the other hand, stayed sprawled where he was, his collar pulled loose and his shirt unkempt.

"Eduard Kozlov made a run for it, but he isn't involved in the case we are concerned with." Out loud, that didn't sound as persuasive as Benedikt would have liked. He continued: "Or rather, he is guilty of leaving that threat on the mirror because our investigation interrupted his drug trafficking, but he didn't put the pen in Popov's throat."

Vodin contemplated the conclusion. His mouth opened.

"So yes," Marshall said from the floor, speaking ahead of Vodin, "we no longer need the handwriting samples."

Without the engine running, the train was alarmingly quiet. Each lull in the conversation emphasized the rustling air outside or the scatter of a pebble being kicked across the floor.

"Correct me if I am wrong," Vodin said slowly, "but you are saying you cannot investigate the murder further?"

They had tried their best. Benedikt and Marshall had thrown the wildest ideas at each other, spent that whole day in the freight carriage thinking about every possible motive someone could have to kill Popov. It was easy enough to come up with those possibilities, but without evidence, each motive was nothing more than fiction.

"I wouldn't say *that*," Marshall replied defensively. "We must be missing something, or—"

Vodin shook his head. "It is irresponsible to keep the train driving if there is no answer in sight. I understand the risk of the culprit escaping, but I must bring in the police."

"But—"

"I have already made contact here," Vodin continued, not letting Benedikt finish his protest. "They cannot get a force out at this hour, unfortunately, so they have passed the summons on to Irkutsk, and we *will* be stopping. The police there are good."

No matter how good they were, though, a train couldn't be halted at a station for long, which meant passengers needed to be cleared off and allowed to disperse. They could do their very best to hunt down the passenger list afterward, but any guilty killer would have made their way far into the city by then. Irkutsk was large and unfathomable. It used to be a center of exile for nobles who had revolted against the tsar. Nothing about the streets there allowed for an easy search; everything from its hand-built houses to its bridges was designed to help someone disappear.

But it seemed there was nothing more to say to change the officer's mind.

Vodin fished his pocket watch from his vest, glancing at the face. "It's almost midnight. Return to your compartment and get some rest. We will arrive at Irkutsk tomorrow afternoon."

As soon as Benedikt woke up the next day, he started to pack their things. It wasn't the end of the world. Even if this particular express rail made its last stop in Irkutsk, there might be another short-distance train that could take them to Vladivostok. They might be able to take a vehicle, use the remaining time they had to drive farther inland.

The problem was that Irkutsk was located at the southern end of Lake Baikal, but on the western side, which meant they would still need to go around before proceeding east. Benedikt wondered if they could travel through Mongolia instead, but that meant approaching Vladivostok from Manchuria, and with the Japanese invasion there, it would be terribly dangerous to travel by land.

He heaved a sigh.

The socks went in the corner. The shirts in the middle, wrapped around the gun he was putting away.

"It is very beautiful outside. Such a shame that we cannot live around these parts instead."

Marshall was hovering by the window. Every so often, he pointed out the little lakes they were passing, the scenery turning more ice-blue the closer they came to Lake Baikal.

"I thought you were reading the directories," Benedikt said, making space at the base of his luggage case. While he was distracted with putting every miscellaneous item away, Marshall had been hovering over the directories all morning. He had brought them into their compartment, lugging each of the five volumes off the dining carriage's bookshelf and dumping them onto their bed. There was one for each year, with the most recent being 1932, issued only this month, and he had been browsing silently. Marshall unspeaking was a very scary Marshall. Under normal circumstances, Benedikt might have been concerned about what he was brooding about, but he had a suspicion that this was Marshall's last effort to find some lead in their investigation, and he knew he ought not disturb any revelations being made.

"I'm staring out into the great unknown to ponder."

"What have you been pondering?"

Marshall pivoted quickly on his heel. It seemed he was ready to share his revelations. "Come look."

He flopped onto the bed, flipping open 1932's issue to the pharmaceuticals section, where they had found Popov's business listed. Then, slowing slightly, Marshall turned a few more pages into another section of listings, for chemists.

"My eye caught on this earlier by complete accident. Call it divine intervention. Or maybe merely my mind operating on a subconscious level, snagging on what it already finds familiar."

Benedikt leaned closer. He had no idea what Marshall was talking about at first. It looked like any old page, a scramble of words and phone numbers and addresses. Then he caught sight of the listing in the corner, giving an address in Moscow and an alternate address in Vladivostok for inquiries regarding the second location, and recognized what he was looking at.

"This is . . . our final destination," he said slowly. Uncomprehendingly. "This is Lourens's address. The one that Roma gave us."

"And yet it is listed as the private practice of someone named Egor Gleb," Marshall said, tapping the information. "Which, might

I add, is the falsest name I have ever heard. Now hold on, it gets more bizarre."

Marshall set aside the 1932 directory. He picked up 1931, keeping the previous book open to the same page. "I figured I might do some cross-referencing. It's a bit hard to go looking for the same *address* in the other books because the pages change around. But since directories are listed by *name*, I went looking for Egor Gleb in every section. He's a chemist in 1931. And in 1930. Same information in 1929." One after the other, Marshall flipped each book open, finding the entries on different pages. "But 1928 . . ." Marshall opened the final book. "I didn't find an Egor Gleb registered under chemists. I flipped over to the previous section, wanting to see if Popov's Pharmacy was gone that year too."

Benedikt peered at the page that Marshall had stopped on. "Was it?"

"Yes." Marshall pointed at one of the entries. "But Egor *is* here. Under pharmaceuticals instead as a private practice. And his Moscow address is the same as the other years, but"—he thumped the newest directory over its edition from five years ago, putting the pages side by side—"if Egor Gleb is the Lourens Van Dijk we know, then in 1928 his Vladivostok address was Popov's present-day place of work."

None of this made any sense. In investigating the other passengers on board, they had been trying to find some sort of connection between a suspect and the deceased. Instead, it turned out the ones with some sort of connection to the deceased . . . were Benedikt and Marshall.

"Do we tell Vodin about this?" Benedikt scratched his wrist. Then his arms, every inch of skin prickling with an unnerving sensation.

"What would we say?" Marshall asked. "'Surprise, officer. If you find any evidence that Lourens has been in contact with us this past year, we're the ones most likely to be the killer'?"

Marshall was right. There was no comprehensible way that this discovery slotted into their investigation. It only sent everything into a bizarre tailspin.

"Then let's forget it," Benedikt decided firmly. He closed all the directories, one after the other. "Pack your bag. We want to move fast once we stop in Irkutsk. We could still find Lourens in time."

Marshall nodded in agreement. While he turned to gather up his clothes and tidy the various items he had flung around the compartment, Benedikt decided to take the directories back into the dining carriage. They were too heavy to carry more than three at a time, so after he put the first three away, he came back for a second trip.

Just as he was holding the remaining two in his arms and pushing out from the compartment again, he rammed into someone in the passageway, making a flurry of motions before narrowly regaining his balance.

The two directories scattered to the floor. As did Benedikt's wristwatch. The poor combatant whom he had struck wasn't as fortunate as he was to remain upright and had sprawled onto the carpet.

"My deepest apologies," Benedikt managed, hurrying forward to give Yeva Mikhailovna a hand up. "I didn't see you there."

"Oh, no, no," Yeva hurried to assure him. She nudged a lock of blond hair out of her eyes. Unlike all the other times he had seen her around the train, her hair was curly today, falling down her back. The sight sent a vague feeling of recognition through Benedikt, though he couldn't place why. It reminded him of someone, but when he tried to identify whom or make sense of where the similarity was coming from, his mind tried to correct him with the usual image of Yeva with her straight hair brushed back.

"I have a habit of ducking my head when I walk," Yeva went on. She looked as if she had just woken up, her necklace dangling over a collar that was nearly fraying into loose threads. "It's a direct contributor to how often I slam into people."

"Nevertheless"—Benedikt got her to her feet—"do accept my apologies."

"Accepted and forgiven. Let me help you with that."

Just as Benedikt was bending down to retrieve the two directories, Yeva picked up his wristwatch. He didn't realize that she was holding it until he had the directories settled in his arms and straightened up again, but by then his hands were too full to do anything except let Yeva turn his watch over curiously.

Benedikt's heart dropped to his stomach. She was staring at the engraving carved into the back of the watch face.

Монтагов

"'Montagov,'" she read aloud. Immediate confusion crossed into her expression. Before Benedikt could hope that she didn't recognize the name, she was already asking, "Like the ones in Shanghai?"

"I have never heard of them," Benedikt lied immediately. He hoped his face wasn't twitching. "I got that watch from a street vendor. In Moscow."

Yeva was quiet for a moment, still staring at the engraving. There was no reason to suspect otherwise, right? Nothing that would give away the truth and reveal the watch as an old heirloom in actuality.

"They are not around anymore, so I suppose that's fair enough," she said. "People say the Montagovs are all dead."

Benedikt's pulse was still racketing with alarm in his chest. He digested her words slowly.

"*People say?*" he repeated. "That seems like you don't believe it."

Either Yeva didn't notice his panic or Benedikt was a better actor than he thought. She offered him his watch back, but seeing that his arms were occupied, she gestured that she could help him secure it onto his wrist. Benedikt angled his arm for her.

"Oh, I don't know about the state of the family at large, of course," Yeva said nonchalantly. She flipped the wristwatch around. "I have only met one of them, most certainly still alive. Maybe this watch belonged to him once. I wish him and his wife only the greatest happiness."

The wristwatch clicked back into place. Yeva gave his arm a satisfied pat.

"Thank you." Benedikt's voice sounded bewildered to his own ears. Yeva seemed to make nothing of it and only smiled before proceeding wherever she had been going before.

As soon as she departed through the doors, Benedikt hurried back into his compartment, setting the two directories on the floor and entirely abandoning his intention of returning them to the dining carriage.

"What was that about?" Marshall asked. He was standing over his luggage case, hands on his hips while he eyed his progress. "I heard bits and pieces."

"I just had the oddest encounter with Yeva Mikhailovna," Benedikt answered. "I . . . think she was trying to say she's met Roma before."

Marshall looked up with a frown. "In Shanghai?"

Benedikt didn't think so. Not if she had mentioned his *wife*, because Roma hadn't married his mortal enemy from the rival gang until the night before they faked their own deaths.

"You know," Marshall went on when Benedikt stayed silent, his attention drifting back to his packing, "you and Yeva kind of look alike in certain lights."

Maybe it was the blond hair creating that effect. Benedikt was still hovering at the compartment entrance, thinking hard. When a full minute passed, Marshall glanced over again, shaking his luggage case around to make more room.

"Ben," he prompted. "You are worrying me a little."

"Isn't it a little strange," Benedikt mused, finally articulating his thoughts, "that Yeva wears a *Y* on her necklace when there is no presence of that letter in the Russian spelling?"

Marshall looked confused. "I'm confused," he stated.

"Yeva," Benedikt said out loud, still mostly talking to himself. "Spelled E-в-a. Mr. Portsmith said she doesn't speak English, so what are the chances that she would represent her name that way?"

"I feel like you're getting to something, Ben. Should I keep making insubstantial remarks until you reach the grand conclusion? That usually works. Maybe she is trying to learn English. Maybe she speaks French instead. Maybe her husband gifted it to her. Maybe—"

"Oh my *God*."

Marshall startled at Benedikt's sudden exclamation. He startled even further when Benedikt rushed toward him and grabbed his shoulders. "Oh my God, Mars, I know what this is. Come with me. Quickly."

Benedikt scrambled through their messy surroundings to find the passenger list, scribbled to near incoherence with their notes. He identified the compartment number he needed, then practically dragged Marshall out, skidding into their carriage's passageway and into the next one over.

"This way, this way."

Benedikt found the compartment. There was humming from inside, stopping only when he knocked quickly, his hands practically shaking as his knuckles came down.

Marshall was right. He and Yeva did look a bit alike.

We met this girl who resembled Alisa to an eerie degree. Roma's voice echoed over from a few months ago, the phone signal staticky. *I figure it was the universe telling me I needed to help her.*

"Your name isn't Yeva Mikhailovna," Benedikt said when she opened her door. "It's Mila Yu."

12

rkutsk's station was fast approaching. The train was about to stop.

"Lev!" Marshall called, spotting the boy as he dragged his bags into the entryway of his compartment, setting them there on the chance they needed to make a rapid exit. "Lev, where is your uncle?"

Lev pouted. "He is in hard-class assuring everyone they can disembark soon. He told me not to listen if you try to persuade me to find him."

"This is incredibly important." Marshall finally got the bags to stand upright, practically gasping for breath from the exertion. He needed to start jogging as a hobby when this was all over. He used to be able to chase rival gangsters across half the city while dodging bullets. These days he apparently couldn't even lift a luggage case without sweating up a storm.

"He also warned me against the lines you would use. *This is more important than anything else. This is a new investigation path. This is a great find—*"

"This is the *answer*," Marshall cut in, waving his hands to erase the other lines Lev had been parroting at him. "Actually, forget your uncle getting his answers. You should want to hear this so you can write about it. My partner is fetching the last puzzle piece."

The boy clearly hadn't been expecting this. He had been standing at the end of the passageway before, but now he hurried closer, his hands coming around his camera eagerly. "Really?"

"It will be the article of the century, I *promise*," Marshall said. "You might even win an award. 'Train Murder Runs Off the Rails with Unexpected Outcome.' There—I thought up a headline for you."

Lev's eyes were big. The bait was set. Marshall just needed to haul the line in.

"No journalist has ever written something like this before. Get your uncle, Lev. Before everyone is forced to disembark and we don't get our resolution."

Without another word, Lev shot off in the other direction. Marshall grinned to himself.

Benedikt ushered everyone into the dining carriage. Irkutsk's snow-covered landscape cast an intense reflective glare outside the large windows, surrounding the train in white as it came to a complete stop.

"Ten minutes, that is *all* I ask," he said to Vodin, pushing the train officer by his arms. Perhaps he was overstepping his bounds just a tad, but they were so close now. He had really only wanted to get Vodin and Lev into the dining carriage—Vodin to report to and Lev so he could get his photos and article content—but other passengers were hearing the commotion in the passageway and were stepping out from their rooms to hear the conclusion of the investigation too.

An audience was fine, Benedikt supposed. He signaled for Marshall at the back of the crowd, and Marshall grinned brightly from where he stood, indicating that they were good and he had the movement under control.

"The police are *waiting*—"

"And they can board very soon," Benedikt said. "You decide when the doors open, right? They will understand that you need a moment to get everything in order. No matter what happens after

I explain everything, they can board. I ask that you just listen to me first. We have spent most of this journey investigating. Ten minutes is all we need now. *Please.*"

Vodin, thankfully, seemed persuaded. Or at least enough to stop resisting. Benedikt released the officer and spun around to look for Marshall again, who was coming through the doors with the last of the curious passengers.

"You got it?" Marshall asked.

Benedikt tipped his head to the side. He had fetched a coat rack from one of the other compartments after cajoling the provodnitsa to let him in. Now it waited by the bar, placed in front of the working attendant, who kept glancing at the growing crowd with confusion.

"I got it. Let's begin."

Lev pushed forward, a pen and a notepad clutched in his hands. He bobbed up on his toes, trying to avoid getting swallowed by the milling passengers.

"Fellow train-riders joining us today," Marshall declared. The dining carriage fell into a hush. "We will waste no time with polite introductions. You have all spoken with us at least once this week while we investigated the death of Danila Andreyevich Popov. Thank you for bearing with us."

Marshall had the sort of theatric voice that could get everyone's attention fixated on the scene. With that done, he looked to Benedikt, who shifted the coat rack forward a little and took over.

"Danila Andreyevich Popov was stabbed through the throat with a pen, in case you hadn't heard gossip about the gory details yet," he said plainly. "He was also a busy man. A founder of a pharmaceuticals company with business in both Moscow and Vladivostok. He made this journey across Siberia often."

"Gentlemen," Vodin interrupted. "I am waiting to hear about the culprit."

"We are getting there," Marshall assured him.

"Right this moment, actually." From underneath one of the tables, Benedikt drew out the briefcase that they had taken from Popov's belongings. He pulled forth the letters that had been bundled in there, mostly set aside for irrelevance in the beginning. "A few passengers heard Mr. Popov arguing with someone, but they only heard his voice. There was the indication of *some* reply being given, but no one could pick out words. No one could guess if it was a man or woman in his compartment—there was nothing to go by."

"And it doesn't make sense, does it?" Marshall continued while Benedikt smoothed out the letters. "We know how thin the walls are. How is it possible to carry on an argument like that?"

"The answer," Benedikt said, "is that it wasn't an argument at all, but Mr. Popov talking to himself. He was writing letters, and he was getting incredibly worked up. He was shouting his argument, then muttering imagined responses from his business correspondents as he wrote his letters. You can read some of these lines and hear the turn in his thoughts."

Marshall shuffled the papers closer to Lev. He lifted the camera dangling at his neck and snapped a picture.

"Next"—Benedikt walked to the coat rack—"for the longest time, we couldn't determine why the coat rack at the crime scene was snapped in half. It wastes several seconds if it was a spur-of-the-moment decision; it doesn't add up if it was a logical decision. Why not swing the whole thing? Wouldn't that make a more formidable weapon because it is heavier?

"The answer . . . ," Benedikt concluded. He picked up the coat rack set in front of them and then suddenly snapped it in half over his knee. The part of his leg that made contact with the furniture piece throbbed in pain, but he drew a few gasps across the dining carriage, and he knew he had made his point. "It wasn't snapped to be used as a weapon. It was snapped in a fit of anger."

"And where would you set it down, unthinkingly?" Marshall prompted.

"I'd toss it near the wall, annoyed," Benedikt replied, as if they were playing off a script, dropping the two pieces closely to imitate the small size of Popov's compartment. He made sure that the top half was positioned just right, the same way it had looked at the crime scene. The train floor was not an entirely flat surface. The top half of the coat rack stayed unmoving because of its irregular shapes. The bottom half started to roll, the circular base taking it in a crescent arc. "Then I would sit down to resume writing my letter."

Benedikt took a seat at one of the dining tables. He mimed holding a pen in front of him. "I am concentrating hard. Furious over what is going on in my work, barely thinking about anything other than the words in front of me."

"Then a knock comes at the door." Marshall thuds his knuckles on one of the other tables. "It is the provodnitsa, checking in routinely."

"So I turn my pen around to avoid its ink dripping while I am not writing." Benedikt gestured for Marshall to throw him a real pen, wanting to have this aspect visualized too, but Marshall splayed his hands in silent answer that he didn't have one. Lev, however, was paying close attention, because he quickly hurried forward, volunteering his own.

"Thank you, Lev," Benedikt whispered. He flipped the ink nib upward. Clutched it in his fist. "I will return shortly to my work. There is no need to set it down." He stood up. Intentionally, Benedikt didn't look down, though a part of the broken coat rack he had tossed was right at his feet. "But the moment I start to walk . . ."

He paused, his foot hovering over the bottom coat rack piece. "I trip and fall." In slow motion, he stepped over the piece. He fell to his knee. "I strike against this protruding piece"—the top half of the coat rack looks menacing now, its hook glinting with danger— "and

I cut that mark into my forehead. Right before the rest of my body entirely loses balance."

Benedikt set his arm on the carpeted floor, elbow at a ninety-degree angle so that his fist was pressed flat, the sharp tip of the pen pointing directly up. The dining carriage had gone silent. Even the attendant behind the bar had stopped making drinks, watching in rapt attention alongside the passengers.

"You can imagine what I am getting at," he finished. "I won't demonstrate the final act."

At once, Benedikt clambered back to his feet, returning the pen to Lev. The boy's jaw was slightly agape, staring in wonder.

No one spoke for several long moments. Then Vodin, his voice almost hoarse: "You mean to tell me it was an *accident*?"

"It makes sense—you know it does," Marshall replied smoothly. "There is a reason why we couldn't find a motive. Why every investigative thread seemed to lead elsewhere instead. There was never a murder to begin with."

The passengers started to murmur. First with barely audible volume, then louder and louder. It got to a point where Vodin needed to gesture for quiet.

Benedikt curled his fist tight. At his side, he felt Marshall shift closer, then reach forward to ease his fingers back into a relaxed state before anyone could see. *Don't be visible about it,* he could almost hear Marshall remind him.

"I'll be," Vodin finally said. He eyed the second broken coat rack, scratching his head. "I will report to the police about this and see what they think."

13

They declined Lev's request to get a photo of them, claiming that private investigators needed anonymity, lest their enemies come after them for serving justice on their crimes. The boy seemed to accept that explanation, because he nodded, then asked for a forwarding address to send them a copy of his article once he managed to get it into print. Gladly, Marshall offered an address and said he was looking forward to reading the story.

The police came on board. Removed Popov's body, then waved in front of their noses at the stench while exiting the compartment, telling Vodin the carpet would need a serious deep clean once the train ran its course. But they *were* letting the train finish its course. There was no need to take it off when there were still passengers waiting to get to their final destination. Anyone who had wanted a previous station could depart at Irkutsk and start to make their way back. The police were perfectly satisfied with the explanation that Vodin had delivered them courtesy of the private investigators on board.

The carriage felt a lot emptier once the train started to run again. Marshall wasn't sure if it was because it had gotten quieter without every compartment at full capacity or if he was imagining the sensation after such a heart-pounding endeavor.

Night fell. When Marshall hovered at the compartment door to watch the train make its next stop at Verkhneudinsk, it almost felt peculiar for the route be running as usual, all the train doors opening to allow the evening mist to permeate into the carriage. The calls of local vendors and kiosk sellers filtered in too, hawking snacks for the traveler tired of the dining carriage selection.

Someone stepped out from the compartment two doors down. Stepan Maximovich Ivanov entered the hallway too, mimicking Marshall's state of hovering.

"I heard that all is well," he remarked in greeting.

"That's one way to put it," Marshall replied. Behind him, inside the compartment, Benedikt appeared to perk his ears, listening in on the conversation while he silently put lotion on his hands. His palms had gotten scratched up from breaking that coat rack.

"I am sorry to have missed the proceedings. It was probably quite the show."

Stepan sounded genuine. There was no note of mocking anywhere in his tone. And yet . . .

"I must ask," Marshall said, making no effort to soften the landing of his next words. "You knew Popov prior to this train ride, didn't you?"

A bout of silence descended into the hallway. Benedikt turned around, quietly creeping closer to Marshall, looking like he was bracing himself in case this question turned ugly. But, two doors away, Stepan laughed suddenly—the sound of someone who had been caught out for a minor infraction like stealing from the cookie jar or running a red tram light.

"Was it that obvious? I was trying to do a good job of not making myself look unnecessarily suspicious."

"The easiest way to avoid looking unnecessarily suspicious would have been to tell us the truth," Benedikt cut in, poking his head out into the hallway too.

"While you were both looking in every direction for a motive? No, thank you. I knew my own innocence; I didn't have to go intentionally shooting myself in the foot. Besides, I put you in the right direction, didn't I?"

Marshall grumbled under his breath, folding his arms. "You could have helped us earlier."

"Do accept my apologies." Stepan looked genuinely remorseful when he pushed a hand into his thinning hair, smoothing his palm down before fetching the hat by his door and putting it on. "To be fair, I did not know him *well*. His workplace in Moscow was just down the road, and I always heard grumbling in my own building about their office leaving the lights on overnight. It truly was a coincidence that I happen to have been able to put a name to the face once on board."

"Nevertheless . . . ," Marshall muttered. He didn't actually have anything to follow that, though. When he glanced at Benedikt, he received a small shake of the head, communicating that they might as well let this go. It sounded like the truth.

Benedikt offered a nod. "Safe travels the rest of the way, Mr. Ivanov."

Stepan tipped his hat. "You as well. Please excuse me, gentlemen— I am off to find something to eat."

He proceeded to the dining carriage. Left alone in the hallway, Marshall and Benedikt exchanged a glance, then both wobbled in sync when the train started to move again, the doors closed and the wheels turning. At this hour, most of the remaining passengers were either preparing to sleep or using the washroom. Earlier, Benedikt had suggested waiting for the train's activity to wind down before they proceeded with their next move. Marshall had agreed, needing a bout of rest after the police exited the carriage.

The time had arrived now. Benedikt swiveled his eyes to the side in a silent question, and Marshall nodded. Together, they stepped out and proceeded to the next carriage. Once again, they knocked on Mila's door.

She poked her head out, looking left and right. Unsurprisingly, she hadn't been present when they were delivering their findings to Vodin.

"So," Marshall began, "now that we've covered for you, care to explain?"

In Benedikt's procession of logic, it had only clicked together when he thought about his conversation with Juliette on the phone, trying to grasp the details of the two kids she was telling him about.

"So this Yulun boy . . . did you mention his last name?"

"No, no," Juliette had corrected. "That's his full name. Yu Lun. He introduced himself a little fast, and I suppose we picked up on the habit."

The *Y* dangling off the necklace. Lourens's connection to the deceased. Every part of this investigation had already been waiting before his very eyes, but he couldn't have put the pieces together until that moment with the wristwatch.

"I will explain," Mila said, closing the compartment door after them. She gulped nervously. "But . . . why cover for me?"

"If you start at the beginning, I suppose I should too," Benedikt said. He offered a handshake. "My name is Benedikt Montagov."

Mila breathed out a visible *oh*. The shift in her disposition was immediate. Suspicion transformed into understanding; tension into inherent trust. She shook his hand. "So you know about the experiments."

"I know that you escaped from Vladivostok after Lourens exited the facility that looked after you. I know they were testing on you but that you have been freed now."

"Well." Mila gave a tight smile. She folded her arms, then walked a few paces around the compartment, looking out her window. The curtains remained open, their heavy checkered pattern fluttering in sync with the movement of the train. "I was freed from their control. I wasn't freed from their attempts at getting me back. If anything, the facility only tried harder because the throat-clawing fail-safe was gone and the man who put that in me was dead."

"The facility," Marshall said. "Popov runs it, right?"

Mila nodded. "Him and his board," she said quietly. "They heard that the experiments had been erased from my body, but they still wanted their subject. The board has always had a sense of owner-ship over the girls they plucked off the streets."

Benedikt grimaced. He stayed quiet, letting Mila continue.

"In these four months, they have sent three separate groups. The moment I circumvented one, the next was already on its way." She pressed her palms into her eyes. "It was no way to live. I was happier than I had ever been, but I couldn't go a day without fear-ing the rug was going to be swept out from under my feet. I didn't know if they would give up on retrieval one day and opt to snipe me from a distance, make it so that if they couldn't have me, no one could. I didn't know if they might switch tactics and go after Yulun instead, use him as a way to lure me in."

Mila took a deep breath. She stayed like that for a long moment, holding it in her lungs. When the train bounced underneath them, she finally exhaled and shrugged off all the frustration evident in her tone, smoothing her shoulders down and tilting her chin high.

"It hasn't hit the news because I was careful about it," she said. "There are six members of Popov's board, including himself. Four located in Moscow. One has gone missing, yet to be reported. One has caught a mysterious disease that will atrophy his every muscle over time. One couldn't seem to brake his car properly, and now he is paralyzed from the neck down. And Popov himself . . . well, I don't know if he realized there was something in the air, but he boarded this train before I could get to him. So I followed."

"We told everyone he was arguing with himself," Benedikt said.

"I have to give credit where credit is due. You didn't leave any trace behind."

Mila looked a little proud of herself. "I wasn't in there to argue with him. He yelled and he yelled, but I only needed him to know which sins he was answering for. He had to know about the irreparable damage he did to me, and he had to realize he was dying for thinking he could ever do that to another person."

"You showed him a syringe." Marshall patted his pocket. The needle piece was still with them since they had never mentioned it to Vodin.

"He got incensed and flung it away," Mila confirmed. "It didn't really matter. At the end of the day, he is a weak man who pays others to do his bidding. He is nothing. Alone in a room with him, all I had to do was pick up his pen and shove it through his throat."

From a rational standpoint, it did come together quite neatly. If Mila had used a real weapon, it would have been impossible to frame this as an accident.

"And then you smacked him with the coat rack so he would go down," Benedikt added. He pointed a warning finger. "That was the one inconsistency I almost couldn't explain, you know. If anyone looked closer, they would realize that the mark on his head runs the other way. He couldn't have gotten it by tripping onto the stand."

Mila brought her shoulders up, covering her ears in a manner that almost resembled embarrassment.

"Sorry."

Benedikt almost laughed. Here she was, apologizing for making it hard to cover up the murder she had committed. The compartment fell into silence. Then Mila leaned up against the wall, fiddling with the curtains.

"Will you turn me in?"

"Why would we do that?" Marshall asked.

A shrug. "Because it's the moral thing to do?"

"Milyena," Benedikt said simply. "We were probably killing people before you were born. We are well and truly the wrong people to expect some moral compass from."

Mila suddenly snorted. "How old are you?"

Marshall folded his arms over his chest. "Twenty-four," he answered for the both of them. "Practically ancient."

"I am eighteen," Mila said, holding back the twitch at her mouth. "I am having a hard time imagining a gun-wielding six-year-old."

"Imagine it, all right," Benedikt said. "That was our childhoods."

Despite his crack at a joke, he did feel terrible for the girl. To be so young and to have suffered so much; to be so young and to have to take her safety into her own hands by playing vigilante.

He cast a quick look at Marshall. Marshall was already glancing back, the same faint distress in his dark eyes.

"What are you planning to do next?" Marshall asked. "Go home?"

"No, not yet." Mila hesitated for a moment. She must have figured that Benedikt and Marshall already knew too much anyway, because she continued: "There are two more board members located in Vladivostok. Once they're gone, then I will go home. I miss Yulun a lot."

Suddenly, Marshall's eyes grew wide. "Wait, wait, you're not off to kill Lourens, are you?"

"No, of course not," Mila answered, sounding offended that he would even suggest it. "Lourens was never a part of the board. He fought Mr. Pyotr at every turn. Roma even said that he was the one who invented the cure, but Mr. Pyotr took it away from him." She sighed, hugging her arms to herself. "I do wonder where he is now."

Marshall lifted a single brow at Benedikt, asking if they ought to divulge their knowledge. Subtly, Benedikt shook his head, communicating that there was no need to bother Mila with the details of their mission in case they only complicated things.

"All right," Marshall said. "Two more murders in Vladivostok to go. That means you're riding to the end with us."

Benedikt smacked his arm hard. Marshall flinched in protest, mouthing, *What?*

Why would you phrase it like that? Benedikt's widened eyes said. Out loud, he added, "And we're around if you need us. Until then . . . I suppose we will leave you to it."

"Thank you." Mila had snorted a little at Marshall's remark, but she still kept her arms wrapped around her middle, like she was bracing herself to remain steady. "For everything. Really."

Benedikt nodded. Wordlessly, he and Marshall took their leave, figuring there was not much more when, at last, they had finished getting their answers.

They didn't speak even once they got back to their own compartment, utterly drained by the day's events. Marshall tossed his jacket off. Benedikt slumped onto the chair. No less than a minute passed before he got up again and took something out of his luggage case.

"One moment. Something just occurred to me."

Benedikt walked back to Mila's compartment. When she opened the door again to his knock, he gave her his pistol, handle-first.

"Vladivostok doesn't make the news much anyway," he said. "Just use a weapon instead of concocting mysterious deaths. It'll be faster and less work for you, I promise."

Vladivostok came into view like a mirage in the distance.

"I cannot believe we spent seven days on a train," Marshall remarked. "It feels like time went by in a blink."

"Only because we were fretting and sweating half the time," Benedikt replied. They were bundled back into their coats, ready to brave the cold of the elements. "You have everything?"

"Yes." Marshall rammed his shoulder into Benedikt's. The woman standing behind them sniffed in warning, jostled by the movement. "I have everything right here."

Benedikt rolled his eyes. He bit back his smile.

The doors opened. A whistle screamed outside. "Final stop! Vladivostok, final stop! Everyone off!"

They moved with the crowd, shuffling forward within a mass of winter coats and fur throws. Benedikt inched off the metal steps first, his boots coming down on solid ground. Marshall was close behind, lugging his bag after him with abandon, almost hitting the passengers behind him as he threw his arms back to embrace fresh air. Out of the corner of his eye, Benedikt caught movement—what seemed to be someone waving at him—and he turned to see Mila making her way down the stairs on the next carriage. Benedikt waved in return, nodding firmly in her direction to wish her luck. She flashed a brief smile and, holding her luggage case close to her chest, hurried off, disappearing with the crowds in a blink.

"Attention, attention!" a station officer was shouting as Benedikt and Marshall tried to push farther along the platform. "The train to Harbin has been moved up an hour! I repeat, the train to Harbin has been moved up an hour."

Benedikt froze midstep. "That's us."

Marshall halted too. "That's . . . bad, right?"

"Depends." Benedikt glanced at his watch. He looked into the distance, at the railway station with its quaint eggshell walls, felt the blow of the nearby ocean salt furling into the city. "We would be getting to Zhouzhuang sooner than expected. But only if we can find Lourens first and make the earlier train."

"Then let's move." Marshall surged forward. "I will find a map. We need to locate a main road."

"You go into the station for bearings; I will find a car," Benedikt decided. "Meet at the front entrance."

"Excellent." Before Marshall could fully sprint off, he spun so he was walking backward, facing Benedikt as he spoke. "We are so good at this. I think we should start a detective agency."

"Absolutely not."

"A missing persons agency, perhaps. I am not picky."

"Mars! Focus!"

With a howl that resembled a battle cry, Marshall ran for the station, a bundle of delight wrapped in a coat. "We would be unstoppable!"

Benedikt huffed a laugh under his breath, pushing toward the roadside. The winter sun peeked out behind a thick cloud, shining bright on the snow. These next few hours would be sheer chaos, but while he charged forward with a goal in mind and Marshall dove along just as quickly, he didn't have any doubt that they could get it done. So long as he had Marshall by his side, the two of them could face whatever was thrown their way.

Together, they were already unstoppable.

ABOUT THE AUTHOR

Chloe Gong is the *New York Times*–bestselling author of *These Violent Delights* and its sequel, *Our Violent Ends*, as well as *Foul Lady Fortune*. She is a recent graduate of the University of Pennsylvania, where she double majored in English and International Relations. Born in Shanghai and raised in Auckland, New Zealand, Chloe is now located in New York pretending to be a real adult. You can find her on Twitter, Instagram, and TikTok under @TheChloeGong or check out her website at TheChloeGong.com.